ORION RISING

LEONARD O'NEILL

authorHOUSE®

AuthorHouse™
1663 Liberty Drive
Bloomington, IN 47403
www.authorhouse.com
Phone: 1 (800) 839-8640

Published by AuthorHouse   06/27/2016

ISBN: 978-1-5246-1616-8 (sc)
ISBN: 978-1-5246-1617-5 (hc)
ISBN: 978-1-5246-1615-1 (e)

Library of Congress Control Number: 2016910513

Print information available on the last page.

Any people depicted in stock imagery provided by Thinkstock are models, and such images are being used for illustrative purposes only. Certain stock imagery © Thinkstock.

This book is printed on acid-free paper.

Ancient Aliens theories say:

In the remote past, evidence was left behind, documented written down, painted on cave walls, in paintings through out time. Evidence that was ignored by the mainstream academics. Some would see this evidence; ask about it, only to be ridiculed for it.

Let me put this idea into perspective for you.

Socrates; a philosopher of great stature even to this day, was forced to drink poison, and take his own life. Because he openly said, the earth was not flat! It was, and had to be round! Put to death for this way of thinking, Let alone out right saying it. So, you see it is not just something so small, as to say Aliens are real at any time in history on this planet! One could be put to death for much less. The motto of most military pilots, some commercial to this day is "If you talk about U.F.O.'s, or say U.F.O. the only thing you will be flying is a desk!" so this as you can see has kept many people from saying anything. In fact, if you asked, the average American in 1975, if they believed in U.F.O.'s the percent was 10%. It has taken until now in 2016 to get that number up to 58% in large part thanks to the men and woman that have dedicated there lived to this cause.

Do you believe in Aliens? Or not?

I ask this to every one.

What If it is true?

What if it all was true?

What if Aliens did come to Earth?

What if they are still here?

What if a couple of people stumbled on to it?

I would like to dedicate this book to:

My administrators at Ancient Aliens group
on face book and soon to be:

www.ancientaliensgroup.com

To all the past Administrators who have
help over the years! Thank you all!!

CHAPTER 1

Mischief

2003 OAKLAND CA. (B.A.R.T.) BAY Area Rapid Transit Station: James Patrick McKandle, 16, brother John Alexander McKandle 18

Sliding down the escalator was not easy these days. The train stations now have the anti-slide plates in between the escalators. One has to get small, cock up on one hip, when sliding down, and hope that neither your pant leg nor your shoelaces get caught. If that happened, it would be a world of pain. "Still the squeaking sound you make while gaining speed is cool" Thought Jimmy as he was almost to the bottom. Then whoosh! Off the end, and hit the ground running. or be run over by big brother John, who was just about five feet behind him. The B.A.R.T. police department was at the top running down the escalator.

Running, Jimmy looks back over his shoulder, even though he heard his brother hit the ground running just like he had, and can now hear his foot falls behind him.

"Which way Jim?" John asks as they run towards the train platform.

"To the right! to the right!" Jimmy yelled back over his shoulder.

Still running, Jimmy looked forwards once again just in time to half knock a woman over who was waiting for the next train. "HEY!" the woman screamed as she righted her self almost falling over.

Jimmy yelled back at her "Sorry!" and kept running.

This train station was, an under ground train station, and John could see that they are just about out of platform. "Jimmy what now?" He yelled asking.

"Jump down, and go into the tunnel!" Jimmy was yelling as he did just that.

They both landed on the tracks, running at full speed, right into the tunnel.

By this time the police chasing them were now four men, half way across the platform, two of police officers saw them run into the tunnel, and stopped running. One of the guards grabbed his radio microphone held to his chest with Velcro. "Central this is Blake, they ran into the tunnel, should we pursue?"

Central responded immediately "Blake DO NOT Pursue! Repeat: DO NOT PURSUE! You've got a train entering that tunnel from the other side as we speak!"

Blake yelled to the other to Officers "Hold up!", "Do not pursue!" even though they could hear the radio as well, Blake did not want any chance of one of his people getting hurt for lack of listening.

Jimmy yells, "Stay to the right! Do not touch that rail that looks like it has a hood on it! That is the Third Rail, and it will kill you!" John looks at it, and the tunnel as a hole and replies, "I know"!

"TOOT!, TOOT!" the electronic horn sound the trains made now, coming from up ahead of them!

"Jimmy! That's a Train!" John yells, not able to see the full light of the train yet, the tracks bend to the right, what looks like a mile or so away.

"Keep running!" Jimmy yells.

TOOT,TOOT! Again this time loader then before, and the light is bending around the corner now as the train is making the turn!

John is running so fast now he is passing Jimmy.

"Were to Jimmy?" He yells.

Jimmy replies, "On the right! That door on the Right!"

John grabs the doorknob tries to turn it…

"Locked! Jimmy!"

TOOT, TOOT!

"Look out!" yells Jimmy as he reaches into his backpack.

John steps back out of the way, and looks at the on-coming train. Noticing for the first time that he can feel the air being pushed by the train, on his face.

John looks back at his brother and asks. "What are you doing?"

Not saying anything, Jimmy pulls out what looks like a computer wire. The kind that attached to the hard drive. On one end was a box of some kind, not much bigger than a cigarette pack. On the other end was what looked like a credit card? Jimmy inserted the card into the slot just to the left of the doorknob. Witch looks like an electronic locking mechanism of some kind. The little box lit up with a row of lights, moving so fast John could not make out any number, it was a blur. TOOT!, TOOT!. The very ground John stood on was now vibrating under his feet. He looked at his brother Jimmy, who was looking back and forth between the on-coming train, and the box in his hand. They both feel the Air rushing by. The ground moving under there feet, now the squealing of the metal tires on the train tracks!

TOOT!, TOOT!

"JIMMY!" John yelled one more time!

Jimmy did not answer, he just kept looking at that box, and then the train, back, and forth so fast, it is a surprise he could see either clearly!

The ground moving faster now under foot, the Air was blowing so hard it was moving the boy's cloths back in the direction of the station! John looked as fast as he could in the direction of the station, to see if anyone was following! Just flash lights, at the end of the tunnel trying to see them. "Thank god!" John thought as he looked back at the train. John realized that the train was so close, there was now way they were going to make it now! "OH GOD!" John heard a sound coming from the door! He looked at the door! The light that had been red until now, turned green, the door made another sound, like a clicking sound! Jimmy turned the doorknob with his right hand, and pulled the card out with his left!

John saw the door start to open in; He just tackled Jimmy into the room beyond. Not sure were the door was taking them, but sure that if they stay here they will be dead! Crashing down on the floor just as the train flashed by so fast, that all they could see was a blur of light, then dark, then light. So fast, they could almost not tell each one from the other! The Air blew so Hard into the room, that papers were flying in all direction. Along with what looked like candy wrappers, gum wrappers, and God knows what. Along with dust, so thick it hurt there eyes to the point they had to close them. As fast as it started it all stopped. John kicked the door closed. They hurried to there feet, looked around the room, and saw a door at the other end of this room. The room seems like a break room, or some such thing, and not that big. With a table, and a few chairs in the middle of the room. Not spending any more time, they both bolted for the door. Jim opened it, look outside both ways. To the right, was nothing, just a dead end. To the left, a long hallway. Across the hall, was a door. On the door was a sign that read "Looker room"; the boys looked at each other, and ran for the door. Going inside fast but not as to alert anyone inside the locker room, they listened, and silently crept in. looking around they saw that they had gotten lucky no one, was inside right now. So they tried some of the lockers "click" one opened. Jimmy was the one that had the luck; the locker door opened, and inside was, slickers, hard helmets, and goggles. John heard the click of the locker door jimmy was opening.

He turned, looked at Jimmy, just in time to see, and catch a Hard helmet flying through the Air, right at him. Followed by goggles! He caught the Hard Hat in his left hand, the goggles in his right Hand, and a slicker hit him in the face! Hanging on his head. Jimmy giggled

4

as he put a hard hat on His head; he was already wearing the goggles. Grabbing another slicker out of the locker he said "Put them on, let's go". John pulled the slicker off his face looking angrily at his little brother for about a second, then smiled and hurriedly put his stuff on.

After making there way back to the streets of Oakland, Jimmy looked around as they discarded there stolen Hat, goggles, and slickers they had, in a dumpster behind some store. "Well, we need a ride home little brother" John said looking around up and down the alley. Jimmy responded with, "yeah no way we can take the train today; the BART Cops will be all over the place looking for us, and the City Cops as well by now".

Jimmy reach into his Back pack once again this time pulling out a cell phone, "I got this" he said while John was still looking both ways up and down the Alley.

Forty minutes later they were exiting highway 242 onto Clayton road in Down Town Concord Ca. located 15 miles East of Oakland, 25 miles East of San Francisco Ca. in the back seat of Timmy McBride's Ford P.O.S., Timmy 18 was driving, little brother Tommy 16 riding Shotgun. "So How did you get that door unlocked Jimmy?" asks Tommy.

"With this" Jimmy says as he pulls out the mechanism he had used, and hands it to Tommy.

"Pretty kick ass! Jimmy were did you get it?" Tommy asked.

"I made it!" Jimmy responds.

Tim looks at the devise in his brother's hand, and then back at the road, "Did you really make that?" Tim asks Jimmy.

John answers for his brother, "yeah He makes that stuff all the time". Tim turns his head, looks into the back set, looks right at Jimmy, points at Jimmy with his right hand, and say "bro you need to teach me how to make that", then looks back at the traffic and puts his right hand back on the wheel. Tommy says "I want one". Jimmy says, "Keep that one, I am making a new one, one that has the Card and two wire clamp as well". John looks at his little brother smiles, and half-asking half laughing say/asks "Wires? What? What do you need the wire clamps for?" Without missing a beat Jimmy says, "Wall Alarms! So I can de-activate all alarms". Tommy looks at his brother who is both driving and at this point is looking back and forth between the road and the back seat looking at Jimmy. Tim looks this time into his rear view mirror and focuses of Jimmy's eyes "will that really work?" Jimmy answers "Yes"!

Tim looks back at traffic for about three seconds and then reaches back to Jimmy with his hand up waiting for a high five, to which Jimmy smacked! Very Hard! All four young men/boys laughed like a bunch of drunken monkeys. As they drove up Clayton road passing the Concord (B.A.R.T.) station. The very one that John and Jimmy had gotten onto to go to Oakland this morning.

Now at home, in the back bedroom of the town house they had grown up in. the two boys are watching the news. Newscaster's voice: Bagdad is being looted! I don't know if you can see this but people are looting the Museum now! It seams like it is organized! Not just rioters going crazy knocking things over! I hope you are getting this! One man, no, wait, more then one man is wired! Are you getting this? They are not just looters they are wired up like secret service! Iraq Secret service but they are dressed like civilians! Jimmy was watching intently, and then looked back at John, who was at the door, with it open a little bit, looking down the hall, and listening to something. "Not the T.V." Jimmy was thinking as he asked John "Are you seeing this?" John did not look at him.

"John, some guys that are Iraq Secret service are taking things out of the Museum!"

John Looked at his brother "What?" he asks?

Then "Turn that down dude! Dad is talking to some guys, and I think they are Military".

Jimmy responds with "SO?"

John closes the door very fast, and pushes jimmy back to the bed "shit here he comes"! "SHH"!

KNOCK, Knock, Knock, "Boy's?"

In stereo John and Jimmy say, "YES, SIR?"

Their father opens up the bedroom door, steps inside the room, and closes the door behind him.

"Boys, there are some Men here who want to ask you two some questions", he said looking at them both back and forth. John looked at his dad remembering what had happened in the train station, wondering, and then asked his dad out right "Are we in trouble?"

"No son you are not in trouble" answered his father.

Then he continued, "You know how I say some times you need to NOT act as smart as you both really are?"

They both nodded a yes, and said it at the same time "YES" remembering that he hated when you just nodded. "This is not one of those times boys", "these men are from the military. They are going to test you both one at a time. I do not want you to hold back one bit, even if it makes them feel stupid. I want you to show them just how smart you boys really are you got me?"

Both boys again in stereo "Yes Sir!"

"OKAY, John you first come with me"……..

CHAPTER

2

Home coming

2007 THANKS GIVING: MOM AND Dads house back in Concord CA Both John and Jim make it home for thanks giving for the first time in a few years.

"Everything smells so good Mrs. McKandle," Jennifer says; "Thank you Jenny!" the voice from the kitchen makes its way to Jenny in the front room setting on the couch with John. They have been dating now for nine months and this was the first time they had met. Again from the kitchen,"you see John at least someone appreciates good cooking".

John yells back "awe Ma you know I was just joking right?" Cindy, on the floor sitting Indian style with jimmy behind her wrapping his lags, and arms around her. Says under her breath to Jennifer "Kiss ass", Jennifer looks at her, then flips her the middle finger of her right hand, and says, "Skank" then they both giggled. John says with a smile, "well I'm glad you two are getting along." to which the girls both looking away from each other almost in stereo say, "Whatever".

John looks at Jennifer still with a smile on his face holds her gaze for a few seconds then looks at the T.V. that has been on the entire time running in the background. Focusing on the T.V. "They say his pass count is getting close," John says looking back at Jimmy.

Also watching the foot ball game now as his brother reminded him of what was happening. Jimmy said "yeah, and if he scores three touch downs it will be his 63rd game doing that and he will break Dan Marino's record". From the Kitchen, "who are you boys talking about?" Jimmy answers her with out missing a Beet "Green Bay Packers, Are playing the Detroit Lions Ma!, we are talking about the Green Bay Packers Quarter Back Brett Farve". Mrs. McKandle responded with' "do you think he will do it"?

John answered this time, "I don't know? He is getting old you know"?

Dad coming down the Hall in a bellowing voice says, "Never Bet against Detroit on Thanksgiving, never Bet against Dallas on Thanksgiving, unless they play each other, then all bets are off!"

He sits down in his chair in the living room facing the T.V. but the chair is placed in such a way that He can see the T.V., the front door, And out the front window with out moving anything but his eye's.

The boys both giggle and John says," no doubt"

They all watched the football game to see what the score was, and who had the ball.

A few minutes go by, dad: one Frances "Frank" Glenn, McKandle asked. "So, how is work boys"?

In stereo John and Jim both say "That's Classified Sir", they smile and John adds "Even from Each other".

Dad looks over his glasses at each of his son's in turn and says' "Dam Strait".

Cindy spoke; "That is silly, what does that mean"?

Jimmy answered, "you see we all three work for the military, in fact we are all in the military, we work in Military Inelegance, however we all work in different places, and on different things. So we can't even tell each other what we do or what we work on".

Jennifer this time, "Not ever"?

John responds, "Never"!

Jim changing the subject looks at John and asks; do you remember all that stuff I told you about from all over the world? Like in central America, Egypt, and South America? All the Pyramids?"

John frowns at Jim, and replies with a question of his own, "Are you talking about (Little Green Men) Again"?

Jim looks back at his brother bothered by his comment "Yes, and they think they are Grey Not Green".

John half-laughing says, "UFO's? People from another Planet?"', "Here?" then laughs out load.

Dad at this point chimes in with, "Hold on there laughing boy, I have seen that new show on History channel what's it called: Jimmy?" pointing now at Jimmy. He follows up with," That (Alien) show".

Looking at Dad now every one was surprised that "Frank" was saying anything like this at all. Jim Says, Yeah it is Umm.. Ancient Aliens!" He almost yelled. From the Kitchen comes mom's voice, "That show scares me! It is kinda creepy!"

John looking at his brother then to his father, then asks, "Mom watches this show as well?"

Dad continues with, "Get with the times John, I read a few books by that Erik Von Daniken, he wrote chariot's of the Gods, back in 1968, Gods from Outer Space, in 1972, I read those two. Another one I have read is The Return of the Gods, 1998, however he has written many others".

Jim chimes in now getting exited,"Yeah he speaks on the show as well"!

John looking back and forth from Jim and his father says "You guys believe everything you see on T.V.? common! You both know better then that."

Then after a short pause, he continues, "AND MOM what are you doing getting mixed up with this craziness?" he yells at the kitchen wall.

Mom walks into the living room now with two bowls one in each hand proceeds to the coffee table. She slides the bowls on to the coffee table, John can see that the bowls are filled, one with potato chips, and the other with what looks like moms Famous Dill dip.

After setting the bowls on the coffee table Sandy "Mom" McKandle, looks into Johns eye, Stands up strait, keeping his gaze, cocks over one hip, tilts her head to one side, then Speaks, "I said it scares me and is creepy, That does not mean I like it, your Dad watches it so I have to sit through it. Though they make a really good case you know, you might want to check it out". With that, she turned and started back towards the kitchen.

Cindy quite to this point on the subject pipes in with

"He had me watch it one time, one guy has a hair dew like some 1980's or 90's, big hair girl on MTV that went Bad. He looks like that guy on the Rudolf the Red nose Rain deer clay Motion holiday thing. You know the one with Mother Nature, Her two sons, one is the freeze guy, and the other is the heat guy? He looks like the Heat guy"

Jennifer starts laughing, she puts out her right hand for a High Five from Cindy and says between laughs "And they had there own theme song to, and his was like I'm Mr. Heat (something)!"

Cindy looks at Jenny, Gives her the High Five while she is singing the first Part of the song and chimes in to finish "Miser! Its I'M Mr. Heat Miser! I Mr. Sun! I'M Mr. something, something 101"! And His Hair stands up like this! She puts both of her hands palms forwards, hands open wide fingers all sticking strait up. She continues to mock the T.V. personality, "and he keeps saying Allegedly, Allegedly, Aliens, Aliens, Allegedly. He is creepy, if any one is an Alien it's that guy!" both girls Laughing now, Jimmy cannot hold back watching the two of them was very funny and they seamed to be getting along for once, he started Laughing as well. John started giggling a bit, even thought it might have been because he heard his Mom giggle from the kitchen.

"You never complained before" Jim was saying as he was giving Cindy a slight shove, and then started tickling her ribs.

Cindy Giggled, wiggled, then slapped Jim's right hand slightly with hers, and grabbed his hand to stop him from ticking her. Still giggling Cindy rocked back words into Jim's chest as if pushing him back and stopping him at the same time. Still with a smile on her face

Cindy looked back at Jim who was now looking around her shoulder to see her face as she was still in his lap, she sticks out her Tongue, jimmy tickled her once again, Cindy Giggled and wriggled but did not fight too hard for him to stop.

"I thought he was Bald" John shot in, still Laughing.

Jennifer half-laughing answered him. "No silly that is the VAN Danikk guy"

Dad not Laughing corrected Jenifer. "Erich Von Daniken, is his name, the one with the Hair is Giorgio Tsoukalos, Phillip coppens has the long dark hair, David Hatcher Childress is the Indiana Jones Guy that goes to all the places and films at the place he is talking about. So you can see what he is saying is true, and it is on the History Channel they do not Have Syfy shows on that channel. They do not say it IS true, in the opening credits they say (What IF it were true?), they are just investigating all the signs that are there, all over the world, that leads some people; that have been to all these places to give Pause, and wonder what all this stuff means? That seems to be the same message, from cultures that had no contact with one another at all. However, they carved the same pictures or have the same creation stories; it is not the same creation story the church is telling us, in fact, they even talk about the creation story of the churches, that they are barrowed from other cultures. That more cultures on this planet have a creation story, which sounds more like Aliens, then gods. Or as they put it, "Misconstrued, or misunderstood, Aliens AS GODS".

John listened to his Father, not saying a word. He looked at his brother Jim, who was looking right at John at this point. Jim nodded in agreement with what there father was saying. John took in a long deep breath, exhaled slowly, as he sat forward on the couch as if to stand suddenly, or as if he was on the edge of his seat. Inhaling again, he finally answered with a question. "And You Believe this?"

Asking the room more then anyone in particular.

He looked around the room now; the girls both said almost in stereo "don't look at me I did not say I did".

Jim looked at John with a strait face, saying, "Brother you should really watch the show", "I am not kidding"

Dad chimed in "Not that any of it Matters, It does not change anything, But If it is real?" "Think about what that could mean?" John stared at the both of them and said "Man you guys are smoking crack, that is just crazy talk, stuff made up to sell Ratings" Jennifer under her breath as if talking only to John said, "That is what I am saying"

Mom just standing there as if she had been there the whole time said "That is enough of that talk can we eat like a family please? And not waste Thanks giving talking about space ships and little green man for Christ's sake?"

"Every one wash up for Dinner" was the last thing MOM said as she disappeared again into the kitchen.

There was of cores no more talk of any kind about that, Taking center stage was the football game and the green bay Packers. On this thanks-giving day, Brett Favre quarterback for the Green Bay Packers would break two records during this game. Not that anyone in the house was a Green Bay Fan or a Brett Farve fan, History is History. In the Win over the Detroit Lions, the Green Bay Packers with a Score of 37-26. Everyone witnessed Brett Farve throw 3 or More Touch Down Passes in a single Game, for his 63rd time in his carrier. breaking Dan Marino's record, Also completing 20 consecutive passes in a row, in a game to break another of Dan's record. he threw for 381 yards in this game, all at the age of 38 which is considered old by most standards of professional football. It was a good day for sports and a great day for the McKandle family.

CHAPTER
3

"Water board him"

PRESENT DAY: 2:17PM WEST COST time. Queen Creek Arizona; less then a mile from town to the north.

About to walk out of the building at the south end of the small Airport like he had done many countless times in the past John McKandle was stopped just short of the door by an Airman sitting at the check in desk. "Colonel McKandle"! John stopped, looked back over his shoulder and responded, "Yes"!

The Guard: "SIR! I have orders to escort you back to the facility". As he stood up, He looked to his right, were two more Airmen were standing. He nodded to one of them, without hesitation the Airmen started moving toward the desk. as the first guard, now looking back at Col. John McKandle, took a step to his left as to side step the desk all together as he did so the now moving guard walkover to the desk and took the first guards place at the desk. "What is this about Airmen?" Asked John.

"Sir I am not at liberty to say, Sir My Orders are to escort you sir", Sir this way please" motioned back to the elevator that John had come out of just moments ago. "Certainly" Col. John said as he started to walk to the Elevator, Pushing the button the Airmen said,

"Thank you sir" the door opened with no ding as one is accustomed to hearing in all public places. The two men stepped in, the Airman pulled out a key as did the Col. on the panel in front of them was in fact no buttons to push only two key holes, to which they inserted and turned there keys at the same time. The Airman commanded first, "Insert", then "Two, One, Turn", and they both turned, this is the time that the Airman would normally quickly leave the elevator before the doors close, however this time the Airman stood fast.

The doors closed, neither man spoke.

The elevator moved fast now, going down, not many floors it always seamed like three or four to John but he could never really be sure. They came to a stop, the door opened; they exited out into a long Hallway. It just moved one way, strait away from them about a hundred yards. John new were he was going, he had just come from here. "Why now do I have an escort?" he was thinking now as he walked the long Hallway.

At the end of the long Hallway was a very large tunnel that ran both left and right of the long Hallway John had just walk. As far as the eye can see in both directions. This, in and of itself, was not a worry to John. As this is the way, he went to work for the last Three years. Setting at the crossroads of the tunnel was a quad runner (Electric, Being in a closed environment they could not run gas) the governor removed it could do speeds up to 65 miles an hour.

An Airmen waited, as was the norm, his job was to just drive people back and forth, there were many of these guys who had this lucky Job. John got into the vehicle, the Airmen stepped on the peddle, and off they went. To the right this time, not the direction that John was accustomed to, He had never gone this way before. "Something is going on I wonder what it is?" John was wondering now as they bombed along down the long tunnel. The tunnel was bright, lights seamed to be every eight feet or so apart, Large enough to drive a tank into, a modern one at that.

The tunnel did not just go strait ahead it seamed to turn left and then right snaking under grown. John did not try to count the seconds as he new they were traveling at about 60 miles an Hour if he counted the minutes he would know how many miles he had gone.

Finally, they came to a crossroads and the Airmen stopped. Three men waited all in suites and ties. "This cant be good" mumbled John almost to laud.

"John McKandle! Could you accompany us please"?

John heard the one man that did not have a coat on, just a shirt and tie. As he climbed out of the quad, John looked at all three men as to study them a bit more. He was not sure, when he would have this chance again. John noted that the three men all had earpieces in one ear. They seamed to have shoulder holsters with guns in them. From the way "Number two", as John was now calling him in his mind, was moving to re-adjust it subconsciously. "Newer guy" Number Two, John noted.

This way please "Number one" motioned. John took to calling this one, "number one" because he was the only one talking, that means he is in charge of the other two. John walk the way he had been lead, down this long Hallway, doors on the right, and left lined the hallway as far as John could see. However, they only walked past three doors before "number one" motioned to the door on the left.

John stopped at the door; "Number three" opened it, and walked in first. "Number one" motioned again for John to enter. Walking in the door John could see it was just a small hallway with two doors on the right side, only two rooms, nothing on the left, or in front.

John knew what this was. He was about to be interrogated about something. He knew what this place looked like, not from being here However, from a different interrogation room in a different place. One thing John did know was that the U.S. Government made things easy with the repetitive way they did everything. It was logical, if one thought about it. If you know one Job in one place, You can do that same job in every place, without having to remember were all the same stuff is in the new place. Or how to navigate an Aircraft carrier if you transfer or loose yours in combat. Second door on the right was were he was going. Yep right on que "Number three" opened that door, and walked in. John fallowed, "Number one" did as well. "Number two" on the other hand, ducked into door number one.

Walking in the door John looked around, not much to see as he had figured a steel table, a chair, more then likely bolted to the floor, and a big two ways Mirror on the right wall. John spoke, "What is this all about"? "Number one" answered him with "Have a seat and we will find out."

At this point as John sat down in the chair that faces the Mirror, as is the customary seat for the one being interrogated, "Number one" said, "My name is, Lieutenant Stanton, this is(motioning to "Number Three") Sergeant Clayton, we want to ask you a few questions. John not trying to be snarkey answered with, "you do realize I am a "Capitan", "Lieutenant"?"

The Lt. responded, I am with "Homeland security" "Capitan" McKandle, So my Lieutenant in fact out ranks your Air force "Capitan" Rank, in fact "Sergeant" Clayton's, "Sergeant" out ranks you, "Capitan". How does that feel "Sergeant"? Sergeant Clayton smiled but said nothing, just looked at John in the eye the whole time. John asked, "What is this all about Lieutenant?" Smiling at John the Lieutenant said. "Okay they said "you were a no bullshit guy, let's get to it." "We both know what this is, you just don't know the why, who, and what for."

This much was true John had no idea why he was being questioned.

Stanton speaks again. "When was the last time you spoke to or other wise had communications with your brother"? This was not at all what John thought was going to be the line of questioning. "My Brother"? "What about my Brother"? Stanton Answered this with. "Now you see John that is not how this works, How this works is that WE (motioning to Clayton and then to himself) ask the questions, and YOU, Pointing at John answer". "So again I will ask you; when was the last time you spoke to or other wise had communications with your brother"?

John responds with "I have not spoken to my brother in a few years. Is he ok"?

Stanton getting visibly annoyed with John. "See there you go again with the asking thing, didn't we just cover that part"? John at this point knew something was very wrong, his mind racing now trying to think what was going on? What about his brother? Did he do something? Is he ok? Missing? Dead? John finally said, (after what seamed like an hour but in fact was about three seconds) "Look I am trying to, and happy to, co-operate with you guys here, you just need to let me know what is going on." Stanton dismissed what he said as if he had never said it. And asked, "you have not talk to, E-mailed, Tweeted, snail mailed, instagramed, face called, spoke on the phone or in person, met with your brother in any way"? "And, you want me to believe this"? John being truthful answered with "yes"! "I have not had any contact with my brother for a few years, and you should know this if what you say is true that you are in fact part of Homeland security". "You would, long before now, even if he took off an hour ago, would have looked into that before we sat down". "So which is it? Are you Homeland security"? "Or Not"? Sergeant Clayton moved the distance around the table in what seemed like a second, grabbed John with both hands by John's shirt, lifted him up, out of his chair, and slammed John into the wall behind him! With more force then John had ever felt one person use on another! He hit his head on the wall, and was sure it was bleeding. The wind was knocked out of his lungs, he was quite sure he was not touching the floor. He could not be positive, as the impact had to his head, vision, and hearing, were good and fuzzy. Trying to breath, and shaking his head to loose the cobwebs. John defensively grabbed the Sergeant back, by his arms. As his eyes cleared a bit he realized that the sergeant was coming at him with a head but! Aiming at the bridge of John's nose! John at this point held on to Clayton's arms, placed both feet flat on the wall behind him (as he was now sure that he was off the ground) and had to time this just right for it to work. John looked at Clayton, and waited that .5 one-half of a second it took, (that seams in slow motion) for Clayton's head to commit! In that, half of a second john waited for the right moment! At the last possible Nano-second John leaned his head to his left, shoving Clayton's shoulders to the right, just a tad bit, Clayton hit his head at full speed on the wall next to John's head! John now with a second to his advantage pushes off the wall with everything he had. As he had placed his feet flat on the wall, pushing with his arms, and legs as hard as he could. In that one stunned second John gained the upper hand, and drove Clayton over backwards on to the table behind him! Before he could do anything else some one more then likely Stanton grabbed him from behind in a chokehold, and pulled very tight! It took less then ten seconds, as Stanton pulled John off Clayton in a choke hold Clayton righted himself, John remembers seeing Clayton looking at him real, real mad! He saw Clayton's Fist coming at him, just before his fist hit John in the face. John thought he saw something in Clayton's eye change, but could not be sure, because that was the last thing, he remembered before the lights went out. With all the fogginess of the struggle John was not sure what he saw, and would probably not remember it when he wakes up even if he wanted to.

John starts to see light… Everything blurry, and sound, muffled, but sounds nonetheless.

Something cold and…. Splashing water on John's Face, into his eyes, mouth, nose, ears, and Lungs With a gasping cough, John gulps down some of the water that has gone up his nose and in his mouth with force into his lungs. He Half coughs and half choke on it! Gasping for air again, John opens his eyes as wide as he can in an attempt to see.

As john coughs, he chokes up some of the water from his lungs. To his surprise he is not tied down at all, it would seem, as he was able to pull both arms up in a defensive position, as to block any farther water from hitting his face, and going into his lungs.

"Ah I see you are awake finally" calls out Lt. Dean Stanton. Coughing up water as he speaks and blinking hard to get the water out of his eyes, trying to focus, John says between coughs "yeah I am up! (Hack, hack, cough) "Listen mom I don't want to go to school today I don't feel so hot" then he giggled still getting all the water out of his lungs.

Stanton speaking again, with much sarcasm "still a smart guy Huh"? "I would have thought that you would have learned better by now Jonny boy"

John just looked at him, then looked around the room, realizing that they were not in the same room that they were in before; oh yeah he felt the pain in his face now remembering that the big guy had gave him a good right to the face. He reaches up again this time to wipe his face to see if he is bleeding. He looks at his hand, and see's blood on it; it looks like he is bleeding from his mouth, nose, and maybe his left eyebrow. Stanton seeing this pipes in with "Yeah Cobb here was a bit ticked off at you for slamming him into that table, so he hit you a few time in the face, even after you were out, he said it made him feel better." Stanton looked past John at this point with a smile. From behind John, some one moved in and put his arms around john and rested his chin on John's left shoulder. "Hey Buddy! You miss me"? Sgt. Cobb Clayton said into John left ear. John shifted his head to the left a bit, and looked at the man with a sideways glance. John Smartly responded "Hey Honey missed you at lunch so I took a nap, How is the back and your forehead?" Clayton growled into John's ear with that comment.

"Okay Lovers!" came Stanton into the conversation again, "Capitan: McKandle, I do not have time to waist here so again when was the last time you spoke to or otherwise had contact with your brother?" John looked at him right in the eye and slowly inhaled through the mouth, as his nose was not working right this second from the blood in it. But responded with "Look I tried to tell you the truth, but you think something else is going on, You think I am lying to you, so we keep doing this, the truth is I have not spoken to him in any way, I do not know what he has done, if anything. I am trying to co-operate with you guys but you just want to hit me, and that pisses me off." with that Clayton shoves John's head from behind as if to say Hey I am still here. John looks at Clayton again with the sideways glance, then turns more towards him and looks into his eyes with a real mad/defiant look. Then returned his gaze to Stanton, looking him square in the eye with the same look.

Stanton looks at John for about three seconds, inhales and exhales through his nose, as he looks from John to Clayton, he says, "water board him". Clayton immediately grabs John from behind in a choke hold, picks him up off the chair, pulling him over backwards, away from the chair, John's legs knock the chair over as he struggles with Clayton.

John took the last moment of the chair movement to get his foot, at least one foot on the chair, pushing off with it, he did get a bit of momentum, just enough to swing his legs down towards Clayton. In doing so started to turn his body a bit, so he is not in the choke hold fully, John uses the swinging motion of his body, now turning away from Clayton, as it swings, not towards him, as Clayton thought he might do. This bought John the one second that he needed. John's feet landing on the ground, he found himself standing, facing back towards Stanton. He all but ran backwards, at the same time with his right hand, grabbed Clayton's arms that are around his neck, not really in an attempt to do anything other then distracted him. At the same time, swung his left arm down, past his own body, as his momentum brought him even with Clayton, swinging his left arm past Clayton, then placed his left hand, Palm flat on Claytons chest. John let go of Clayton's arms with his right hand, slipped it under Clayton's arms. Taking a long stride with his left leg, John is able to position his left leg in front of Clayton's legs. With his palm still on Clayton's chest, John pressed as hard as he could against the mans chest, at the same time shoved his hand into Clayton's armpit, with his fingers locked together he shoved them deep into the mans body as hard and as fast as he could. Jabbing a nerve cluster, that hurts more then getting kicked in the groin, if done right, it feels like a knife stabbing you. This had the effect John was looking for Clayton loosened his grip just enough that John was able to slide his head out of his grip. Now John pushes off with his own right leg, in an attempt to get Clayton off balance. He pulls on Clayton's shirt now with his left hand, this rocks Clayton as he knew it would. Clayton's momentum at this point took him over John's left leg, witch was now tripping him, as his knee twisted as John stood now with his left leg, and leaned his body back towards Stanton. Clayton could do nothing but flip over John's leg and land very hard on the floor. Just then, the lights went out! Not sure, what was going on John moved in the darkness back in the direction of both Stanton and the door to John's left. The door crashed open with a bang, John turned to see just were Clayton was, and to avoid the bright light at the same time. Then real bright flash and an explosion lucky for John he had looked away just then to find Clayton, it was in fact a flash bang! When John turned around again it was over and full darkness again he could see the door, did not know were Stanton was. Glad the flash bang had not affected him so much. He headed for the door. As he got to the door he wondered why no Stanton? Though figured he had blinded himself when the flash bang went off. He ran out the door, not looking back. John looked for any door that might lead outside, to his surprise; it was rather easy to find the way out. As he approached the open door to the outside John could see that a man was just outside to the left of the door, he did not see John sneaking up on him fast. John just stepped up and punched the guy in the side of the head as hard as he could, the guy just dropped like he was hit by that UFC Fighter who knocks every one out. Although he could not remember the name right now, He looked around and took off running not even sure what direction he was going in. as long as it was away from this place, John did not care just yet. Running this way, and that, John was not trying to figure out were he was, or at least what direction he was going. John heard something behind him! He stopped dead in his tracks. Even stopped breathing for a few seconds to listen. Crack! Someone was out there; they just broke a branch or twig! However, they were out there, and looking for him. John at this sound turned away from the sound and took a step to continued running but nothing was there! Just air! Down John fell! Tumbling over rock, and brushes he fell about 10 feet, then hit the ground, hard and sprawled out on his stomach! "Oh that hurt!" he said to himself as he began to stand. With a grunt he stood up, looked forward just in time to see two bright lights,! And hear the screeching sound of tires skidding! Oh! Sh*& John tried to jump, or maybe he didn't, He would never be sure! Upended rolling and bumping up, over, and off the back of the car and once again hard onto the ground, that John new now was in fact Asphalt. "Oh man that hurt" John thinks as he lays there for a second. Then remembers what is going on. John knows he has to get up, and get up now! He stands up in doing so makes sure that nothing is broken or at least not to badly broken, still not sure he turns to see who hit him hoping it was not either Stanton, or Clayton. A woman runs up to him! Oh! My god! Are you ok!? She is looking him up and down as if trying to see if he is broken or missing anything. John says "What?" she answers with a question "are you okay?" John looks in to her eyes and answers her "NO!", "you just hit me with a car!" He was a bit rummy so he shook his head to clear the cobwebs then realizing she was not Stanton or Clayton. John said, "Hey Listen you have to help me please they are going to kill me", moving towards the car now as he is speaking John continues, "common we gotta go like now! Get in, lets go, you drive; yeah you drive I was hit by a car! So you should drive" common lets go before they get here"! He said as he got into the care. The woman looked around, did not see anything but herd something so she to jumped in the car, and took off real fast. Driving as fast as the car would go, away from the scene. Neither person in the car saw the three men in black, watching as the car started to leave. Then disappear as Stanton, Clayton, and another man, poked there heads out of the brush that John had fallen from. Clayton said, "I got the plates", "Good," says Stanton lets go find them.

Back in the car, the woman keeps looking at John and then the road again. John is looking him self over as well. She breaks the silence first "are you ok?' John looks at her, and responds "No" I am not ok" I just got hit by a car. Before that I was beaten, choked, maybe water boarded, and I think I was drugged, but can't be sure, because my head is fuzzy but that might have been from getting run over by a car". "Although they did hit me in the head as well". "I am bleeding from many places, however I don't think I am broken at least I don't feel like I am". John now looking at the girl driving remembered that she was the person that hit him. He says, "Hey you hit me with a car, why did you hit me with that car?"

She could tell that he was in shock and my have a concussion she says, "We need to get you to a hospital"! John looked at her for a moment then said "No! That would not be good", "then those guys would find me", "why don't you just pull over and let me out here"? She looked over at john as if he had just turned blue then spoke "Are you crazy? You are in NO condition to be walking around in the dark by your self, and just how did you get in the middle of the road like that"? John did not answer; he had passed out about 10 seconds ago. "CRAP! Crap!" she said, then "No! No! You don't get to just do that! Stay with me!" she was screaming at John now "STAY!" she reach over and slapped John's face Hard! A few times. John came to but was not fully awake as he said "You know you guys are starting to piss me off you know, Keep hitting me in the head like that and I am going to have to tell you what I did with your sister the other day", "hahaha" then out again he goes. She slapped him a few more time yelling "common!" John opens his eyes again. They are rolling around in his head, he says, "my answer is still the same, not going to change even if you did him me with a car, is that all you got? Common man I aint got all day!", "I got things to do and people to be, frat boy, you hit like my grandma", "give me that week ass shit meat!". then out again, the women realized he was not going to die, she actually thought he might be sleeping not passing out, then she thought about what he just said, he thinks I am them and he has still

24

not given up fighting, tough S.O.B. she said out load. John responded by asking "Can I have some water?", "thirsty", out he went.

It was a good thing that she kind of knew the area she was able to find an emergency room at this time of the night way out in the dessert of Arizona, some place called Ironwood.

4

Tuff S.O.B.

WAKING UP JOHN HAD TO get the fog out of both his eyes and his head. Looking around at what looked like a hospital room; John started to get up, and was in a lot of pain. He tried again, everything seemed to work nothing seemed broken but was stiff, and hurt like he had been hit by a car. Then John asks out load "was I hit by a car?", and realized he said that aloud and no one was in the room but him. Tossing back the bedding John swung his leg around so he was setting in the side of the bed now. AAHH! As he moved, John realized for the first time he was wired up, an I.V. on the back of his left hand and heart monitor stickers all over his chest. "Crap!" he thinks knowing if he messes with them an alarm will go off. He pulled at one of the small wires hooked to suction cups on his chest, he plucked the cup right off of is chest, immediately an Alarm sounds from the machine to his right all the wires seam to go back to this machine he quickly lays back down and pretends he is asleep. A nurse comes in, goes over hits some button and the alarm stops. John opened an eye just enough to see what she did to make it stop, then closed it again.

The nurse went back to what ever she was doing off to the right of John's room, He could hear her talking now to the other nurses, Though he could not make out what they were talking about.

Not wasting any time John quickly sat up, and started pulling on all the wires. The alarm started to sound, John was ready for it, and hit the reset button as fast as the alarm made a sound, and it was so fast the machine did not make much of a sound.

Sure, that no one would have, or could have, heard that machine, John now worked on the I.V. that hospitals put in you, as a rule, even if you do not need or want it. Now adept at resetting Hospital Machine John also disarmed this one with great ease.

As John stood there pulling off the last of the suction cup, stuck to him warring only his socks, and underwear. The door started to open! John's Heart raced! "It could not be the nurse I can still hear her off to the right!" John thought.

Moving toward the door, Getting ready to grab who ever came through the door.

The door opened about a foot and stopped. John froze in place. A Man popped his head in the door, he had a dark green, ball cap style hat, it looked military but not at the same time. Before John could react, the man spoke! John, at the same time the man was moving his right arm in, and extending it toward John. Taking a defensive posture John held his ground, reading himself for a possible fight.

Take this; the man said, extending a cell phone to john.

Answer it when it rings, find some cloths, I will distract them. John did not move fast enough for the mans liking, he tossed the cell phone to john and was gone as fast as he came.

The phone rang; the volume was almost all the way down so the sound was very faint.

"Hello" John almost whispered.

"John it is me!" A voice on the other end of the phone was saying.

John was about to ask whom this was, and then it hit him; it was his brother's voice. Man I am glad to hear from you there is some real craz... that was as far as he got when his brother interrupted him."

I know you don't have much time listened to me!" Find cloths! And get out of there as fast as you can! They are coming for you! Go!! Move now!"

John asked "were to?"

His brother answered "Out of that hospital! ", "we will do the rest just get out and do it now!"

In just underwear and socks with a cell phone in hand, John opened up the door very slow and looked out in both directions. Moving to the left away from the nurse's station, John started down the corridor looking at the door as he did so, he finally found a maintenance closet, and inside he found some maintenance cloths so he dressed like a janitor. Put his phone in his pocket and headed towards finding the way out.

As John rounded the first corner, He could help but to look back down the Hall towards the room he had just left. Coming from the elevators at the other end on that Hallway was five guys moving real fast and Armed! They quickly burst into the very room that he had just left hastily thanks to his Brother Jim's Phone call. Not to be seen john moved out of site, and hastened his pace to find a way out of this place as fast as he could.

Not knowing were he is only that it is a hospital made for a difficult time finding the door out, without being seen.

He moved from hallway to hallway looking both ways like a scared boy about to cross a busy street.

John finally came to a Hallway that had a sign on it that read: Lobby; with an arrow pointing to the left, Emergency; with an arrow pointing to the strait ahead on down the hall. Radiology; with an arrow pointing to his right.

John looked to his left. He could see the lobby down there, the door that looks like it leads to the outside.

He also could see the Policeman, military men, and the woman that had hit him all talking in the lobby!

The decision was made for him in an instant, Emergency it was! He moved with a purpose.

"Look! Officer! Like I told you before, He was on the ground in the middle of the road that is all I know! I Helped him up, into my car and then Here"

The woman that had in fact hit John, and then helped him was saying for the umpteenth time, and getting a bit angry at all the questions.

The Military guy now piping in again with a question.

"And what did you say you were doing up on that mountain again? Miss?"

Seeing between the police and military officers, she saw movement down the Hall. Out of habit, she focused on the movement. In that split second she could have sworn that was John, now she was sure it was. Looking at both the men in front of her, she said, "Look! I Need to use the restroom ok?" as much telling as asking them.

"So just hold onto your horses for a bit I will be right Back"

The police officer Nodded, as the military officer said, "No I think that..." he was cut off by the police officer holding up his left hand waving him off. He looked into his eye with the look of "do you really want to go to that place with a woman". He fell silent and she walked toward the direction that she had seen John go. As soon as she reached the Hallway to turn left were John had gone she hurried around the corner, No John, she ran as fast as she could down the Hallway.

At the end of the Hallway was a sign that read Emergency: with an arrow pointing to her left, and Radiology: with an arrow pointing to her right. Figuring That John was heading for the outside she turned left and sprinted again. The Hallway ended and turned to the right. she came to a stop, looked to her right, this time she could see the emergency lobby, people in it, and more importantly no police!

She could however see John looking around and at or out the door! She hurried across the room, right up behind John. "There you are"! She said startling John!

She grabbed Johns Arm, leaned in real fast, and kissed his cheek.

"Lets go we are going to be late"!

As she held onto his arm, she turns toward, the door, half dragged John, as much as not all the while moving through the door out to the emergency Parking lot.

"WHO?" John barley got out before she said under her breath. "Quite","Move" very stern.

Then followed up with "We gotta go and now".

Moving a bit faster now she mumbled to John again.

"My car is this way keep up".

John noticed it was still night, cool but not cold. He looked around a bit to as much see if anyone was following as much as to see were he was.

He saw a sign that read IRONWOOD medical center.

John thought "wow I am still in Queen Creek, well just outside of town"! Then thinking again "I was under San Tan Mountain the entire time, and must have been were I came out if she brought me here".

"Get in" the woman said as she opened the car and was getting in her self.

John hurried into the car, she had it started before he was all the way in, as fast as she could the car was in reverse, pulling out, in drive, moving to the exit of the parking lot. She turned right and hit the gas!

"Who are you" John just got out when he realized that they did not have any lights on, and she was driving really fast! Not answering the woman asks John "you still have that phone"?

John looked at her, his mind racing fast now! "Yes" "Yes I do". He said

"Give it to me"! She ordered as much as anything, putting out her left hand, all the while keeping her eyes on the road. John looks from her to out the windshield and back noticing they were going even faster now then before. He reached into his right front pocket, pulled the phone out, and handed it to her. They must be doing over a hundred miles an hour now with no lights on straight out into the desert south of Queen Creek toward San Tan on N. Gantzel rd. If he was not mistaken.

The woman took the phone in her right hand, swung it around in front of her eyes so she could see both the road, and the phone at a glance. She pressed on the phone with her thumb a few times, held it up to her right ear. John could hear the phone calling a number, and then a voice answered. "I got him" she said.

"We are heading to you E.T.A. two...." that was the last thing John remembers her saying. As he was looking at her to his left, John saw movement just out of focus out the driver side window. As the movement came into focus and before John could react. He realized it was a black SUV moving at about the same rate of speed as they were only it was not passing them it was in fact, and did crash right into the side of the car!

5

He is Chipped!

EVERY THING SEEMS TO SLOW down to slow motion like in a movie as the black SUV's impact caused glass to fly every place. Airbags deployed from every direction, he was driven to his left as the car was driven to his right. At the same time the woman was moving in Johns direction being pushed by both the airbags, and the car itself. As it was being folded in from that direction from the impact! Her right hand and arm was pushed off the stirring wheel by the air bag, it met Johns face about half way. It was like as if she had backhanded John in the face. Followed close behind by her head, her hair was the first thing john saw, it was not very long. In fact, kind of short, brown, and he was not sure if it was her or her hair that smelled like Vanilla. However, he would not remember this fact until later as her head slammed into his. She let out a small sound like she was in a lot of pain, but could not scream. The kind of sound you make not on purpose, due to the impact of when you fall to the ground, and flop right onto your stomach. John then found that he to made this same sound when followed by her head was her body slamming into his. The two were now being crushed into John's side of the car, surrounded by airbags! The car was now rolling to Johns right away from the SUV that had struck them. Just how many times the car rolled over John was not sure, in a split second it was over. The airbags deflated, they were upside down, the sound of parts, pieces, glass, and who know what was hitting the road coming to a rest in any and every place all at once.

Before John could breathe or assess what had just happened, he heard the sound of metal being forced to move! Then some one grabbing him, pulling on him! Then he was out of the car! His eyes not quite focusing yet. Blood in his face, coming from his nose mouth, forehead, John was trying to focus on what was going on right this instant. A second or two later John realized that he was being dragged by his caller! The Man was saying something though John's ears were ringing still he could not quite make out what he was saying. John shook his head like a prizefighter trying to shake the cobwebs out of his head. He leaned back, looked back, up to see who was dragging him, most importantly, what was he saying.

Shaking his head, again John was able to see clearer now. He looked again at the man who was dragging him away from the wreck he was just in. it was Cobb Clayton! And he seemed pissed off!

Cobb was mumbling as much as talking to John when he said. "Make me have to come all the way out here! Wreck a good SUV to retrieve your dumb ass!"

John looked back at the car he was in, it was upside down, and in fact wrecked really good with a black SUV still smoking and dripping some fluids all over the road hissing and popping and some other noises that don't sound right. Both vehicles were totaled.

John heard the sound of tires screeching as someone was driving really fast and stopped even faster, then he could smell the smoke the tires made as the burned rubber down on the road. John tried to stand up or move in a way to get to his feet.

He grabbed Cobb's hand and try's to turn him self over to get up. At the same time, Cobb stopped pulling John, and as much helped John to his feet as John did to stand up.

Cobb still had his left hand holding Johns shirt by the back of his neck.

Cobb turned around and yelled "HEY!" at John!

Then with his right hand slapped John across the face, then pointed at John's face. "HEY!" Cobb screamed again, "I am tired of your shit!"

John reaches up, and tried to break Cobb's hold on him.

Cobb responded buy jerking him, and yelling at him again "HEY!", "NO!" pulling John again toward the second SUV that had just arrived.

Then from behind, someone crashed into Cobb with enough force to nock loose his grip on John! Cobb goes down to the ground with a thud!

Landing just past John, hair covering her face slightly matted with sweat, blood, and glass, was the woman that John until now had not dared to think was, in fact alive, and real pissed off! Taking a stance like a person well versed in Martial arts, she walked toward Cobb.

Cobb rolled real fast forward at the woman! stood up strait, both hands clasped before him like as to make one big fist out of the two, thrusting them at the woman's face, in one move that John had not seen any one do for some years. She side stepped to her right, spun to her left, took one-step forward putting her self all but standing next to Cobb facing the same direction as he was. While doing this she had positioned her right arm up flat in the air with her elbow bent palm down in front of her own face at the same level as Cobb's face. Swinging her elbow backwards, she cracked Cobb in the mouth with enough force to knock his head back, stepping backwards as she did this putting her right foot next to Cobb's left foot. In one motion she changed direction with her left arm, rolling forward, down, around under, and behind Cobb's left arm! Pulling on his arm now, she dragged his body leg to leg, hip to hip to her left. Cobb before he could think was up off the ground balancing on the woman's hip, with a text book hip toss she flipped Cobb over and slammed him down on the asphalt, onto his back so hard John thought Cobb was a goner for sure. Cobb hit the ground so hard he made a sound both pain and the wind being knocked out of his at the same time as his head bounced the second time on the ground, there were gunshots!

John jumped with the sudden sound of gunfire!

Second SUV had three Men in it and they had guns in there hands firing back behind John at something or some one, before he could turn to see what or whom two of the men were shot! Blood shot out of one, as the bullet went through his neck, the other man just dropped to the ground as he was hit in the head, he just went limp. The woman also stunned by the gunfire stopped moving, and looked up. Cobb still on the ground grabbed the woman by her arm and pulled her past himself toward the gunfire behind both he and John, rolling forward again, Cobb was not moving away from the gunfire back to the SUV. The third man now opened up with a machine gun spraying a very large volume of bullets back past John, he was now moving the rifle from his left to his right! This meant that he was now spraying the whole area and laying down suppression fire John knew if he did not duck, he would be shot! John hit the deck, the woman did like wise. John could not see behind him still but got the impression that who ever was back there did the same. Cobb ran, down past the man spraying the area with bullets, and headed for the back of the SUV. The third man followed Cobb backing away while he continued to fire!

A voice from behind John yelled "John! Rain! Move!" John thought he miss heard the man he knew he had meant "John! Run! Move!" however, it sounded like he said "Rain" in any case John got to he feet, head down, and ran toward the man! As he did so he realized that, he knew the voice! It was his Brother Jim! The woman also jumped to her feet, she got to the men just as John did, though she did not run past them like John did, to take cover behind the SUV. She instead stopped, as a man held out an M-16 she took it, turned around and open fire back in the direction of Cobb! Just as this was happening a third SUV, from the other side pulled up behind the other two! One wrecked, one left abandoned now as Cobb and the other man had backed away from it as the now third SUV pulled up. The doors open two more guys hopped out, guns blazing. John noticed six people in it, Cob down two men, had four. Cobb reach inside the SUV then back out, pulled the pin on what looked like and in fact was a hand grenade!

Cobb rolled the grenade under the SUV they had abandoned!

"Grenade!" John heard Jim yell! Every one hit the deck!

BOOM!! The SUV exploded in a ball of Fire! As this was happening Cobb, and his men, all loaded up in the surviving SUV. They bolted into the night as fast as they could! All lights off! Jim yelled "Load up they will be back in a hurry!"

"We need to Buggout fast let's move"!

Looking at John, Jim said, "Let's go brother"

John hopped up, Hurried into the SUV.

With out missing a beat everyone loaded up in the SUV Jim being the last one in. he and John sat in the first set of seats, the two up front were men John did not know, then Jim, and his self, next row was a woman, and the woman that had just fought Cobb, followed buy two more men in the third row seats.

No lights on inside or out of the SUV they drove blind in the pitch black down the desert road! Only the occasional street light. The driver asked," Can I get a heads up display please"?

The second woman in the seat had a laptop open, she was typing on it. As she answered "working"!

Then all the windows front, sides, and back blinked. Then in an instant light up with a soft orange/red imaging that John had never seen before. John was astounded! It was like nothing he had ever seen in his life! Like a night vision only not green or black and white! It was this soft outlines in this orange/red clear as daylight imagery. "What the heck"? John found himself saying out loud. Still looking around at all sides as he did so. Jim said "yeah I know huh?"

"This is cool shit".

Then the woman with the laptop pulled out something, held it up to the woman next to her and moved it around her as if she was scanning her some how. Waving her hand all around her. The laptop beeped. She stopped, said "clean"! and click some buttons on the laptop, then reach up, moved her hand at Johns head, she clicked a button again, and waved her hand around John leaning forward as she did this. She got to Johns waist and the laptop mad a different sound then before! A red light came on!

"HE IS CHIPPED"! She yelled! The driver said "SHIT"! Jim moved fast now and said to John "pull up your shirt there at your waist!"

John did what he said the girl waved her hand again and still a beep and red light! "Paints!" Jim shouted!

John pulled down the waist of his pants again she waved and again a red light and Beep!

The passenger watching this now said! "SHIT"!

Jim said to John "This is going to hurt Brother" as he stood up as much as he could in the SUV.

"Lay down on your side" the woman said to John.

He did as she said. She handed the laptop to the other girl, reached under the seat, and pulled out what looked like some kind of med pack, all Black, with many pockets and compartments. She tore open the top with the sound of Velcro ripping when pulled apart. She grabbed something and sprayed it on the area she had scanned. It was cold on John's skin.

Putting that back she pulled out something else.

The other woman now waved her hand over John in the spot that the beeping is. She said the other woman "It is not deep"! The first woman replayed with "Good" as she pressed a button on some device she had pulled out. To john surprise a laser red in color was cutting into his body like a knife, there was a little smoke coming off the spot as it cut John open.

She did this to a length of about 1/8th of an inch. To his surprise, it did not hurt.

Putting this device away, she pulled out yet another device. This one she pointed strait down at the open wound. This little tiny arm like thing came out of the front strait down and into the whole. Just as it did John saw a small claw like thing made of metal open at the end and then gone inside of him now.

John could feel it grab something and now a beep from the laptop the other woman said "got it" the girl holding the device pulled it out slowly.

When she got the device all the way out it was holding onto something that was still attached to John. From the inside! "What the?"! John said as he watches this unfold.

She then pulled out the laser device again still holding the other device in her left hand she had the laser in her right hand. "This may hurt a bit", she said then turned it on and cut just below the little metallic thing that she was pulling out of him.

It cut loose, she then handed it to the other woman, then her left hand now free she pinched the incision back together with her left hand and pointed the laser thing at it and now the light was closing the whole not leavening any scar! As soon as she was done doing this, the other woman was waving her hand now at him all up and down. A beep and a green light later she yelled "CLEAN"! Everyone in the SUV seamed to relax a few of them even let out a long load sigh of relief.

"What is that thing"? John asked.

The woman held up the device with the little metal piece still clasped and now bloody.

"Tracking device"! It runs on your body's natural electrical current it will die in a second or two.

John looked at the object then right into the woman's eye's and asked "what"? Then "wait"! "what?!"

Then John sat back in the seat looked at his brother and asked "what in the heck is going on?!"

Jim replied with "I know! A lot!", "I have a lot to tell you, I am sure you have a lot of questions", "AND, you are not going to like it nor believe it" !

He continued; "I have tried to keep you out of it John, However it has gotten to a crazy level now".

"INCOMMING" the woman with the laptops said rather loudly not quite a yell.

Jim Look at her and asked. "what type?"

"Choppers times two!" was the response.

"Direction?" Jim asked.

"North!, Moving south, FAST!" she answered.

Everyone except the driver and the woman on the laptop looked in that direction. They could see two search lights coming down out of the sky. It almost looked like it came from no place. What ever craft was shining the light' was very dark against the night sky.

The drive spoke first, as he glanced in the rear view mirror. "We need to go Dark please"

Without looking up from the laptop the woman was typing real fast now as she said in a calm voice, which seams to have a tone that said (you bothering me is slowing me down!)"Working on it!"

Jim still looking in the direction of the helicopters asked. "anything else?"

The woman not missing a beat said. "Not so far"

She stopped typing, looked up, and said. "Wave goodbye to the nice chase vehicles" she pressed the enter button! As soon as she did this, John got the feeling that something had happened, like a wave washed over him and the entire SUV! Though he could not see a change, the air had a faint smell of electricity, John was sure his vision had detected something as well but could not put his finger on it. He looked around; everyone seamed to think this was fine. He looked at his brother and asked. "Do you smell that?" Jim looked at John with a smile answering. "Yes I do my brother, yes I do"

The woman with the laptop then said. "We're good"

"What was that?" John asked no one in particular.

Jim did not answer he asked a question instead. "Still not sure about all this John?"

John looked at him for a second or two, then looked around the SUV at everyone, then asked a question of his own. "Okay what is going on? ", "you got my attention".

"What do you mean you lost them?" Cobb was asking. "How in the Hell could you loose them?"

He continued.

From the other end of the radio, a man replied. "Sir, I am not sure how, All I can tell you is they were there then they were not!" when we got to the spot that they were there was no trace of them".

"Okay keep looking for a few minutes then get back to base." Cobb said as he pulled out his cell phone, and dialed a number. The phone rang only two times, the voice on the other end said. "Be advised this is an unsecured line, this is lieutenant dean Stanton"

Cobb said only three words "They went Dark"

"Rodger that" was Lt. Stanton's reply they both end the call just like that. Cobb looked at the driver and said. "Back to base". as the driver turn the SUV around Cob made another call on his cell this time he said "we need a cleaner out here, two vehicles, a few bodies ASAP, coordinates as fallows"........ The SUV drove off.

Ancient Alien theory

FIRST INTRODUCTIONS: JIM WAVED A hand to the front of the van, our driver here is Kendle. "KIWI" smith he can drive or fly anything. Kendle appeared to be about six feet tall; he has blue eyes, blonde hair fare skin, no facial hair, although he does have earrings in both ears. Next to him in the front is "DRAKE", "we don't know his real name," Jim said, "and don't ask". He was a well-built man also blonde hair blue eyes, though his eyes are a darker shade of blue then Kiwi's are. No facial hair, no earrings, he was quite. John had not heard him speak so far, accept the cursing when John was chipped. He was about six feet tall as well. Jim then turned sidewise to his left the girls are and waved his hand again pointing this time to the one behind John "RAIN" you know, she hit you with the car, and then crashed it later! HAHA by the way are you okay? I never did ask yet. Jim looked into her eye's for the first time, John could tell he meant it, she looked back took in a deep breath, "nothing broken sir"! Jim still held her gaze for about three seconds, then said "OKAY", "but I want "DOC" to look you over when we get there", he looked at John, pointed at John, and said "you to! Have "DOC" look you over make sure you are ok, you have been through a lot, I don't need you falling out now we just got you out."

"Rain" was about five feet, 11 inches tall, brown hair, blue eye's small tan.

Now waving his hand again to the row of seats right behind, he pointing again, this time at the woman that had done the bug removing on John. "This is Kelly she is one of our hackers, if it is electronic she can hack it. If it is programmable, she can program it. She is like KIWI in that he can drive of fly everything, she can work, hack, program, decipher, or control anything electronic. Her street name is "SMOKE" her Hacker name on the Net is "SHADOW". Kelly also was about five foot eleven inches tall, blonde hair, blue eyes. The guys in the back, as Jim pointed again first to the man on the left. This is Daniel breakwater,"WINDWALKER". Our linguist, historian, he can translate everything, even if it is not from this planet. Jim smiled as he said, "Daniel", he was about five foot nine inches tall, jet black hair, brown eyes, and darker skin. Though his hair was short, John got the impression that he was very Native American. His name did imply it, more over he looked it.

Jim nodded this time to the last person John had not been introduced to, this is Ron "OVERLORD" O'Graddy our sniper, explosives handler, and weapons master. All around badass "RAIN giggled", no one else laughed. "That being done" Jim was saying, "Lets get down to what is going on and why, I am sure you have a ton of questions, right?"

John looked at his brother and nodded as he answered, "Yeah I surely due". Jim started;

"Okay, do you remember when we kids? Dad and I watched the show on T.V.?"

John not fallowing asked "WHAT?", "T.V. SHOW?"

Jim continues; "yes, "Ancient Aliens", we watched it all the time. We even talked about it at thanks giving"; "Do you remember that"?

John was now thinking real Hard he took a deep breath in and then let it out, and asked "UFO's".

Then went on to ask; "Are you telling me that this is about UFO's"? "Because that is just nuts Jim you know that".

Jim looked at John right in the eyes, and said, "Look around brother, look at what just happened"!

"All of this! Everything".

John thought about it for a minute. Then asked; "drugs? weapons? secrets?" what are we talking about Jim"?

Jim looked disappointed at John, then said, "That is what you got from all of this?", "Let me ask you a question John?", "When they interrogated you what did they say I had done?"

Jim waited while he watched John thinking…

Then followed up with "They didn't did they?"

"I bet they never once accused me of anything?"

"did they?"

John thinking back on the last few hours could not remember them ever saying anything about any one thing or another. He answered Jim "They never said, the just kept asking me when I had seen or spoke to you last"

Jim looked a John for a few seconds without speaking as if waiting for John to think of something. Then asked "what did they say?"

John answered, "They just kept saying you are in trouble, you are missing, what did I know about it?"

Just then, "Incoming!" the woman with the Laptop said. The driver spoke back to the rest of the team saying; "They Know we are in the area!", "They are phishing now!" Jim called out "we to go off road they will not doubt watch the road", the woman on the laptop called back

"Make a left at any time" "That is due east"

With no hesitation, the driver did not slow down at all just turned left and went off road, Due East!

"Okay" Jim was saying to John. "You are not going to like this but it is the truth", "UFO's are Real", "Aliens are Real", "Everyone in the world knows about it except Americans".

John Looked his brother right in the eye's, again took a deep breath in, and let it out. Then said; "NO!"

Jim looked at his brother for a few seconds, then said; "look around, what do you see?"

Then before he could answer he continued: "I know you have been through a lot today, however look around you, right now and tell me what you see going on right now" John glanced around.

Jim was moving his hand now pointing at the windows. The heads up display on the windshield, and asked, "How do you explain the tracking device we just took out of you?". Not waiting for John to answer, "What about the technology we just used to get detect and retrieve it? Let alone the heads up, or the laser was used to get the device out of you?"

Again not waiting "Explain any of it".

John answered "New cutting edge tech. High tech stuff we have all kinds of this kinds of thing in development".

Jim responding "really?', "you have seen it or worked with it?"

John looked at Jim now for a good long few seconds then spoke; "Proof"?

The only word he could think to say at this point.

"I can't show you proof here", "we need to get to a buggout safe house, that is were we are going now"

"I will tell you what I know."

"There are a few theory's out their in the world. Which one is true is not as important, as the fact that there are more then one. The first, and most fallowed is, tablets that were found in the desert, along with the Dead Sea scrolls, in Samaria, which is modern day Iraq, and Iran. The scrolls said that the "Annu naki came from the sky. The words mean "those that came from the heavens". They came for gold it was hard work so they decided to create a labor force. One that was simple minded, and could be controlled. One that they could tell they were Gods. They blended the DNA of a primate from here, with their own DNA; this created a race of humans. They told them that there job was to mine minerals for them. They left after some time, tried to kill

44

off the race by a giant flood, not all died. Then a second race came to Earth later, this one was also a human race. But one from a different place. They saw that something was wrong with the human here so they up graded them with there DNA! This upgraded the humans to were we are today. There are like I said other theories out there. Also others that say none of that happened. Still more that say we evolved to the human we are. That when the U.S. government started seeing along with other countries, lights in the sky. They then started realizing it might be people from another planet. The U.S. government shot down, or made them crash, on purpose to gain technology. That we did do just that. That we have many Alien people, ships, technology that we have reverse engineered. We are conducting experiments on our own people, by blending our DNA with that of the Aliens we kidnapped and there is now UFO's flying around because it is us.

And yet still, another theory that says; both happened, both the U.S. government and Aliens are playing with our DNA, and they are giving us Technology when we look away. In addition, others all saying that there are Aliens here, on this planet! A shadow government is working with them, and there are many Alien Races among us!", "the one thing that remains a constant in all of this, is; one thing, Alien race, or Races, are here now on this planet!"

John looked at the group one by one, taking his time doing so, then back to Jim, and said one word "PROOF!", "You don't have any Proof; everything you are saying to me is science fiction"! "Not Fact!"

John thought about it for a moment, the asked "And you all believe this nonsense?", "No wonder they are looking for you?"

Jim did not answer he instead looked at the woman with the Laptop and asked her "How are we doing with that incoming?"

She was tracking the laptop screen the whole time they were talking. The replied "Clean so far, they do not seam to be detecting us".

Jim looked and John but said to her "Good", then said to John "Look I said I can't Prove it to you here, just think about what I said and get some sleep you have had a hard day and we have a long way to go"

They drove on strait out into the open desert heading east.

45

CHAPTER

7

South Mountain Base

JOHN HAD JUST REALIZED THAT he had fallen asleep at some point however could not tell how long he had been sleeping. He started to move, everything hurt! "Wow he was stiff ", he was thinking as he sat up right from the slumped over position, he found him self in. as John's head cleared, he realized they were still moving. Then thought to himself "well why would you not be in pain John, you got in a fight, fell down a mountain, got hit by a car, T Boned doing 75, and shot at!" That will do it!"

The sun was just coming up now. John looked at Jim who was watching the road ahead. He could hear the guys in the back talking now, low not really audible.

John Rubbing his left shoulder, while rolling his head about his neck to UN-stiffen it at the same time.

He hears Jim say. "You know you really are lucky you did not get killed with all you been through"

John just answered with "Right?"

The SUV slowed a bit, John saw for the first time that they were in fact not driving on a road.

They came to a stop in front of what looked like a small fifteen by fifteen foot square one story building with a tall wire fence around it with both barbed wire and Constantia wire at the top, Bars on the windows that he could see. Drake the passenger hopped out, unlocked the gate, and moved it out of the way; Kiwi drove in and continued to the right of the building. Behind them Drake swung the gate closed as they passed clear, then re-locked the gate and jogged along behind the SUV. As the came around the back of the building John saw that there was four more SUV's hidden buy the building it self from the front, then realized that was the back not the front of the building. John asked the air again "what is this?"

Jim answered. "You'll see"

Kiwi pulled the SUV along side one of the other SUV'S they are all lined up side by side. Everyone out, Jim called as he opened his door and started out. John fallowed Jim even though he did have his own door. Everyone had duffle bags, everyone that is but John. They all filed up to the door Jim walked up to what John could see was some kind of pad. Jim placed his right thumb on one spot then leaned in and put his face up against another one John new this was scanning Jim's thumbprint, and the other was scanning his right eye. John found his mind racing "What the Hell was going on?" a buzzing sound and the door made a loud clicking sound. Jim grabbed the door pulling it open he held the door open like a doorman would and waved everyone in. John just stood motionless as everyone brushed past him to disappear in to the small building. As Drake jogged up one of the guys had grabbed his bag and tossed it to him as he to brushed past John, with this John and Jim were the only two not in the building. Jim looked at his brother, smiled, and said "common", as he nodded into the building.

John at this point took in a breath, then let it out and he walk in to the building.

In side now John could see it was not well lit inside, along the right wall was a set of stairs that went down at a steep angle, in the middle of the room was what looked like an elevator, Kiwi had his thumb on the one button on it. With a "DING" the door opened up and it was in fact an elevator, everyone took turns getting in, turning around and facing the door.

Jim, then John again last one in.

Looking at the controls of the elevator, John could see just four buttons open, close, emergency, and one very well worn button that hade nothing written on it. Jim pressed this button with his thumb. The doors closed, and the elevator began to move.

Down was the direction they went, elevator picked up speed at first then settled at a good rate of speed, then slowed right at the end of the trip just like a normal elevator. In fact the whole thing reminded him of going to work in Queen Creek. Once the elevator stopped, the door opened to a room that just had the staircase on the left that ended in this room, the elevator that also ended in this room, and another door directly in front of them. Jim stepped out first; he walked over to the door just like before, putting his thumb on one pad and leaning in for his eye on the other. "BUZZ,CLICK!" this time as Jim pulled on the door it was real, real thick when this door final swung open it had to be At least four feet thick!

"Wow"! "Big door!" John said. "Just like work" John looked right into Jim's eyes now. Jim smiled and explained. "That is because this is in fact an old nuclear missile silo" it was bought by a company we hold, and sold to a man by the name Ben Sherman who is in fact Daniel's great uncle, they call him "Blackbird". The natives still do not cotton to making the family stuff public to the U.S. Government so they do not know they are related.

John looked through the door, saw another elevator he looked at John and said "really?", "how many time are we going to do this?" Jim smiled did the same as before with the thumb thing and eye.

Elevator came they went down, this time when the door opened it was only a large command center bustling with people, military personnel. John look astounded as he looked around he saw at least ten people. John not looking at his brother asked. "How many people are here?" Jim replied. "Here only about twenty, this place in fully contained sealed air tight. The tube that the missile was in has been re done. The lower fifty feet is fresh water. The area above that is five floors of eco system, we grow our own food. All the air is scrubbed, even the generator that give us electricity. The carbon emissions are put through a scrubber, and contained so we do not breathe it. The generator runs on bio fuel that we make from olive oil that we grow here. We could house fifty people in this facility for just about ever if we had to."

"Wow" was John's response.

"And you all believe in this UFO, Alien stuff"?

Jim looked real Sirius in to John's eyes then answered. "YES"

"There are more"!

John's eye's got big as he asked "what do you mean, MORE"?

Jim still looking very Sirius had a flash of doubt for about a half of a second as he thought "Man what if we are wrong about him"?... then knew it was his brother.

Finally said. "Yes it is not just me and a few of my closest crazy conspiracy friends, running loose like a pack of wild dogs John. There are thousands of us, tens of thousands of us all over the world." that fear flashed over his eye's again. Then he stopped. Right then John heard a voice he would have never, ever would have thought he would have heard here.

"Yeah John there are many, many people involved in this". John turned to see his very own Father looking at him. Stepping out from behind him was his mother.

CHAPTER
8

More Ancient
Aliens evidence

WHEN COBB GOT BACK TO base, he went inside to check in with LT. Dean Stanton USMC who he had spoke to on the cell phone a few minute ago.

"Sir" he said as soon as he saw the LT. also snapping to attention, and saluting the LT.

Dean waved off the salute, and then replied. "Come with me", then turned and started down the hallway to his left, Cobb fallowed right on his heals. Speaking as they walked. "The brass has realized this is bigger then they first thought, so they have put together a unit to deal with this". Cobb hearing this asked a question. "Good for us?"

Stanton stopped dead! Did not turn around, glanced over his left shoulder at Cobb then,"Yes and no" then began moving again. At the end on the hallway Stanton grabbed the doorknob of the last door, but did not open it right away, he looked back at Cobb and raised both eyebrows up and down at the same time as if to say, "Are you ready for this?"

Then opened the door and walked in with Cobb Fallowing.

The room was big, set up like a war room, it had a lot of people in it, Cobb stopped moving, looked around at all the people, Stanton sensing Cobb's no longer following him stopped, turned around to face him, smiled, then said with an exited look, "yeah! This is the stuff!" Cobb smiled and began following again. They walked to the center, of the back of the room. Which was up a bit of a ramp, raising this spot above the rest of the room. So that from this spot, you can see all other spots in the room. You still see the giant display board in the front of the room, with out any one in the way if they are standing.

As they approached, Cobb could see three men standing at the spot in the center of the rise all in uniform, all in different uniforms. The one he notice the most was the highest-ranking man in the room, which is in true military tradition to identify the highest rank then on down the line so no mistakes take place. This one being a navy Admiral!

Then two colonel's one air force, one Marine!

As the approached the men, Stanton spoke, "SIR'S!"

He then stopped snapped to attention and saluted, not missing a beat; Cobb did like wise, one-step behind, and to Stanton's right.

The officers looked up from what they were doing, the marine officer took a step forward, snapped to attention, and saluted back, only then did Cobb and Stanton drop Salute, as the Col. Did.

"Stanton and Cobb Sir!" Stanton said.

The Admiral looked at them. He spoke before anyone. "Cobb!"

Snapping to again Cobb saluted the admiral and replied. "Sir!"

"AT ease son", the Admiral was saying, then, "what happened out there?"

Cobb answering, "He had help, Sir, His brother showed up in force".

The admiral continued; "Yes I am aware of that, we were tracking them, and then they went black, can you explain this?"

Cobb did not hesitate. "It would seem that they are far more sophisticated then we first thought Sir"

At this, Stanton spoke to Cobb. "Cobb this is Admiral Jerry Bares USN, colonel Jake Persinsky USAF. Colonel Timothy Poe USMC.

Cobb answered the Admiral, "I believe they are more then just a few guys Sir".

The admiral continued' "Any theories?"

Before any one could speak, a woman that had walked up behind Cobb in uniform spoke up. "They are many! And they are being helped! Sir's!"

Cobb turned to see who this was. Before anyone spoke colonel, Persinsky spoke up. "Gentleman!, this is lieutenant Tina Collens USAF".

Lt. Collens continued. "To find, and remove the tracking devise in John, was one set of technology, to go dark was another one all together, Sir's".

Cobb spoke next. "When they extracted John they did not try to run during the fire fight Sir, they were not afraid, nor did they act like they were in a hurry, had we not pulled out Sir, I believe, they were in the fire fight to win it! Sir's".

LT. Collens again. "We have had our eyes on a lot of other personnel, and civilians Sir's that we think may be involved" "though we did not have the resources to follow up Sir" this time she was speaking directly to the Admiral.

Admiral Bares answers her directly, "Well we do now!", "We now have as many personnel as we need"!

Colonel Persinsky spoke next. "These guys are acting without the authority of the United States of America, or its Military services, they are acting outside the law. That is treason, possibly Sedition!"

"We need to find them!, figure out how many other people are involved, and squash this before it gets out of hand!"

He looked around and everyone nodded in agreement, with this Lt. Collens spoke up. "Sir's if I may? In the matter of putting together of a team? Without running the risk of being over pretentious, I should handle that task. In the interest of two many chiefs not enough Indians, as it were. We have one admiral, two colonels, we don't need any farther high ranking Ego's to deal with. Maybe what we need here is personnel that are; how shall we say? A little less courier minded, and a little more lead able?" She finished with a smile on her face; the three officers did as well. Stanton and Cobb glanced at each other side ways and smiled a sheepish smile.

The admiral then said "See to it LT." to which she replied "aye Sir".

With that LT. Tina Collens turned towards Stanton and Cobb, "Walk with me boys" she was saying with a smile on her face like the Cheshire cat, as soon as they were out of ear shot of the three high ranking officers Tina spoke again "Now, we get to put together a proper team! The less of them we have on it the easier it will be for us" Motioning back to the three officers as she spoke. "Now Boys get us some real Fire Pissers so we can find, catch, and deal with this rabble".

"Mom? Dad? What are the two of you doing here?" John was asking, as he then started looking around expecting to see everyone he knew.

His Father spoke first. "Son there is some thing you need to listen to, and I mean really listen to!"

John looked at his dad then his mom and asked "you to?"

John's mom looked deep into his eyes before she spoke. Then started,"Son, I know I do not have my head completely wrapped around all of this yet. But I am starting to, and it is not from any type of brain washing!", "our Family is to strong for that, you either have the facts, or you don't. You either believe the facts or you don't.!" Johns Father piped in "I know all of this sounds Crazy, Crazy! However, hear them out, and keep this in mind even after, What if? What if it is all true?"

Jim said "ok let look at things from the beginning", he motioned to a monitor and said "Here, sit down and take a look". John walked over and sat down in the chair, took in a deep breath, let it out slow, and said "Okay lets see what you are talking about".

Jim started with "it is Long, I will try to make it short and to the point, archeologists', scientists', and historians all over the world in the modern era have been looking for the answer to who, how, when, and why are we here, even before them throughout time, Right so far?" John answered,"yes"

Jim continued, "Okay, in the past, things have been overlooked by academics. Because it did not fit into the ideology, they were selling. Until the 1900's, and even after that, for a time, one could be put to death for going against the grain, on some things. like in the 1900's, we were just a few Hundred years away from people believing that the Earth was flat, and that the sun circled the Earth. People were put to death for saying that Earth was not Flat.". "in the early to mid 1900's, a man by the name of Zecharia Sitchin, supposedly translated some scrolls that were found is Samaria. some say he translated them wrong, though these people that say he was wrong have never come up with a version that differs his to show he was wrong". "that translation said that the (Anunnaki) the word means {Those from the Heavens came down} created humans by using there own DNA and blending it with the ape of this planet to make a worker to mine for Gold, Diamonds, and other raw materials, this work was hard and the Anunnaki did not want to do it".

As Jim was saying all this pictures were on the screen showing the progression of the story.

Jim not missing a beat continued;" Okay lets toss that out, and say the people are right about the translation.", "take a look at this" Jim started showing pictures again on the view screen.

As he spoke the narrative, "you know about the pyramids' in Egypt right?" he glanced at John then to the pictures of the Giza plateau. John answered with a simple "Yeah" Jim continued, "Scientists believed that they were made about three to five thousand years ago. Though modern testing of the stones used place it much farther back in time. As far, back as one hundred thousand years ago.

Let's toss that out as wrong" at this John said "you are so far giving a strong case that it is all bull brother, why?"

Jim looked at his brother, and started again, "I am showing you how absurd, and narrow minded people are," "so, we have found that all over the world in countries that as far as we know, that did not have any way of speaking to, the cultures from the other side of the world. No influence what so ever did not trade with or interact with. However, we find some thing repeated over, and over, and over again. By cultures that never had any contact" pictures on the view screen again, each one coinciding with what Jim was saying. Pyramids, some sloped like Egypt, step pyramids. almost identical in width, and in Height uncovered, all over the world, Peru, China, Iran, Iraq, Indonesia, Polynesia, Sudan, Mexico, Cambodia, Italy. Even in the United States, when asked, who built them? The native peoples would say the gods or the star People, or the ski brothers. Drawings of a human man, with the head of a bird, holding something that looks like a purse. On his wrists, something that looks like a watch, or smart watch. Holding what looks like an acorn. In his right hand, extending it like, handing or delivering it. Wings on his back. Every time the pose, the stance, the clothing. Every detail is the same, even facing to the right".

Jim continued cycling through the different counties and showing the Image of the same creature, or man, or God. Then continued. "Also, more images of a different would be God". He begins again, this time with a new face. This face was on a small thin-bodied person. Around four foot tall. With an oversized head, that was Bald. It had no ears, small slit of a mouth, almost no nose. But for two tiny holes. However, the eyes were larger then a humans eyes. They are stark pitch Black, olive shaped, coming to a sharp point just at the nose. The skin was a grey, leathery look. As Jim scrolled the pictures the variation was very slight Jim continued to call out names of countries, times, and places, for what seemed a very long time. "It seamed that it was in every country throughout almost every time period, this little guy." John thought to his self.

Jim stopped the images, and said. "There is a mathematic equation out there as well however that can go both ways, I say this about all that, if there is a God and this God made the entire universe? However, did not make any other life other then on this planet, and we are the only intelligent life in the universe why waist all that space by putting us so far out on the edge? For one: why not make the universe, and the sun revolve around us? For two; why would God give us a low mortality rate?", "okay even without all the complicated crazy algorithms, and far over complicating fuzzy mathematical far reaching crap. In the Drake equation, hundreds of billions of stars, If only one planet per star? That number is so low that is un-fathomable by the way, but let's say one." "The odds are that any planets in that group will achieve the {(goldilocks Zone) this is the not to hot, not to cold, but just right! For life to evolve} are more then two, a lot more then two." "However people have been programmed to deny this notion at all cost even to the event of murder or suicide", "with the advent of social media humans are being educated at a far greater rate then any other time in the world's history. With education comes knowledge, with knowledge, comes wisdom, with wisdom, comes understanding, then comes perception. all of this combined is allowing us to start to fight our programming, to question, even the small control the rich think they have over the poor. People are beginning to wake up, and perceive the world for what it really is. To see for the first time what is going on, truly going on. This is scary for some, terrifying to others, still others are not afraid. Only that we are not in charge like we think we are." Jim smiled then finished,"That is the short of it, there is much, much more, but that is the essence of it in a nut shell".

All of this swirled around in John's head.

He was trying to wrap his head around what he had just looked at and heard from his own brother, his mom and dad are in on it. As he thought "Oh man!", "This can't be happening", My Mom and Dad?", "What if?", "Little Green men?", "No little GREY Men, how convenient", "we are programmed to fight against the truth at all cost", Also convenient does not allow for disbelief, if you deny it, it is programming". Finally John said out to the room," I need more proof!", "Bigger Proof, why has no one seen one like a Bigfoot?' Jim responded "Because the government has grabbed them all up and threatened everyone involved to silence", I told you that there is more". Frank (the boy's father) spoke at this point. "Jim that is enough for now let him assimilate what you have told him so far. He needs to make sense of it before he can go on, it is not like us, we have been looking into this stuff for year it is all new to him".

John got up from the chair he had been in and walked around the room a bit, Looking at the people around him, what they are doing, Seeing that they believe what they are doing, none seemed off the rocker, they look like any other situation room he has ever been in, and that he knew was quite a lot. John noticed that the room and all the equipment looked like a cross between NASA, and the President's War room. All the same seriousness hustle and bustle, professional accuracy one would expect to see from military personnel doing there job, more over believing in it.

"Proof" John was thinking again, "Proof, Proof, and Proof!"

Ant people

THE FIRE WAS WARM AGAINST the cold night air, every few minutes the pine wood, would pop as the fire got to a sap pocket, it would crack, Embers still red hot would float up into the high desert air. Little turtle looked into the fire. Watching the flame dance around, and the smoke coming off of it. He held a large stock of white sage in his left hand. The end was smoking, it was smoldering. In his right hand, he had a feather of a bald eagle. He was waving the feather directing the smoke of the sage, and of the fire first towards him self. Then away from him self, he was setting on the ground. He looked around at the two men he was with, waved the smoke at the men. With this he stood up arms stretched out wide, smelling the air, he started to chant in the beautiful Native American fission. Not to loud, still enough to move a mans soul. He pulled his arms back in close, fanned the smoke, while blowing on the sage to stoke it.

He is a Hopi shaman buy the name Little turtle or Earth Dragon as some know him, 48 years old raised the Hopi way on the reservation, the two men with him are his son "little eagle", and Little turtle's nephew "yellow feather" both 24 years old, they have been on and off the Reservation most of there lives however have embraced the Hopi way.

Little Turtle stopped chanting, looked at the men and said,"the time is close, we must make ready things for the time is coming, and again the Hopi people must once again take a guiding way. It has come to it!" "We must sleep now and in the morning we must make are way to prepare, we must tell the elders!"

About a hundred miles to the north-west from were the Hopi shaman stood is a place called "The four corners" it is literally a point were four states converge Utah, Colorado, Arizona, New Mexico, what people do not know is that in that place in an ancient native American Indian reservation! Located and surrounded by first the Hopi, and then the Apache! However in the middle right close to the "Four corners" in the Anasazi tribe. Some ware near the four corners at almost the very second that little turtle felt, and knew that something was coming, an Anasazi woman, a shaman of the Anasazi people was reading a book, an ancient book, she to at the very second sat bolt up right! She is a young woman, in her late twenties. The woman known to her people as white fang, had a new name, one that was given to her in the ritual that made her the shaman of her tribe. The name was given to her as the shaman goes, so to walks a new person in the skin of the old. She was not entirely sure about this new job she was chosen for, not sure, this is what she wanted to do or be. She loved her native people; she loved her native ways, the culture, the history, the mythology, and still not sure. That is until this very second, you see; as she was reading the book she had not been looking around the room. She was settled in for the night, one lamp still on, the one she is reading by. Before she knew it, the walls of her cabin had gone, no longer a cabin, she was in fact setting in the chair next to the lamp in the middle of the woods, at least that is what she saw when the first movement caught her eye. She looked up over the book, expecting to see the other side of the room maybe something moving outside had caught her attention;

however, no Wall was in place. All four walls, the roof, floor, carpet, furniture, all gone. What she saw was native warriors dressed in ancient Battle gear, in fact they each one whore the skin of a wolf, the head of the wolf on top of there head like a hat or Helm. She counted fifteen men, with spears, bows, arrows, and knives. They were moving from her left to her right, in front of her about twenty-five yards away from her. They moved as if they were tracking some one. One of the warriors was looking up at the sky often, as much as they were the ground. He seamed to be in charge, he called out the other men, and they stopped. She could not quite make out what was being said, even though she was fluent in Anasazi. She did not move a muscle, not sure, if it was fear. Or if she did not want to disrupt the event or if it was even happening.

She just held fast with book still in hand looking over the top of the book.

The men set about gathering wood; "lucky that none seam too interested in this direction, on this is still not real" she found her self-thinking.

As soon as they had the fire going, the lead man pulled something out of his bag, it seamed to be some kind of dirt or ash. He tossed what ever it was into the fire! With this, a great PUFF of Smoke! And a flash! All the men now watching the fire, and smoke coming off of it. The Head man walked around the column of smoke until he disappeared behind it. As soon as this happened she heard a whoop! Come from the fir! Or, maybe it was from the headman who was in fact behind the fire, and column of smoke from her point of view. With no warning! The Man came flying through the column of smoke, as if he had jumped over the fire but through the smoke.

He landed facing her though still not looking at her he turned around to the other men encouraging them to do the same. One by one they took turn first with a Whoop!! Then through the fire. As they landed, they looked as if they stood guard almost protecting the fire light it was a door or portal! As the last man jumped through the smoke, they all stood back to the fire as if protecting it. Looking to the sky as much as the land all around them. It was only at this point that she had noticed that the headman was now looking right into her eyes!

Her Heart raced as she almost felt his eye's as much as could see them. Not in a bad way, however the could see into her very being.

Finally, he motioned to her with a wave of his hand as he spoke "Shadow Walker! (Using the name, no one knew that was given in ceremony) Come witness this!" She was not sure what to do at this point! Then she thought to her self "Okay, you are a shaman of the Anasazi Tribe now"! She got up from the chair leavening the book to rest on the seat of the chair. Shaman; {Shadow Walker} of the Anasazi Tribe was having her first vision. Making her way over to the Warriors' she could feel the forest around her, Smell it, hear it, see it, it was cold in this spot, though the fire helped. "Come see this!" he was saying again.

She walks right up next to him, he was taller then she first thought, as she stopped next to him he said, "Look, see what the Hopi and Anasazi have seen in the past and foretell". She turned around expecting to see the way she had come, forest, and the chair she was in, However as she turned she realized that was not the case, the chair was not there, the trees, and the hole forest was gone in a blink of an eye! They were in fact not in any kind of forest at all! They were atop a Butte in the middle of the desert! It seamed to be the four corners area. All around in every direction. She could see something in the bright day sky, something shimmering against the blue of the sky, possibly metallic it was a long way off yet. The man pointed to the valley floor. She looked down to ware he had pointed. A long way off, she could make out a craft, like she saw in the sky. On the ground by the base of a butte. Not to far away from them. Lots of people running to that point, many people. as many as thousands, in a big hurry to get to that point, out side the silver almost reflective metallic vehicle or craft was people waving the running people on. He people kept running she looked back in the sky; the one that was far away was now close it moved through the sky with grate ease. It seamed to move too fast from one place to anther, then back again. Shadow walker did not like the feeling she was getting from looking at this flying, she exhaled in a long deep breath, and thought" no, that is not the word I want to use because that is crazy", instead she thought the words, and even said them out loud "OH MAN!" A sinking feeling filled her; she looked down at the people running, for the first time really under stood what might be going on here, the people made it in to the cave before they were found out. The other vehicle flew away also undetected.

The Head man, as she was calling him in her mind, because he was in charge. While watching this scene unfolding, pointed to the cave entrance, the people are running into, and said, "Ant people". "Ant people help all". Then continued, "It was said that some time ago, long ago thousands of years ago. First came a flood, then ten thousand years of ice! It is said; that the ANT People came, like now, help our people in caves. In these caves, our people lived for ten thousand years. Until the ice melted, then they lead us out into the world again." "Time is coming again".

She new this was true to what she had read, heard, and been told. Now seeing it before her was something all together different.

As see was thinking it the Headman said "come we need to go before we are detected". Shadow Walker turned to head back to the fire thinking she would need to jump like they had. Found her self standing in the middle of the room, of her cabin facing her chair as if she had only stepped a few steppes away from the thing. All the walls, roof, floor, everything was as it had been, only a few moments ago. Though she could still smell the headman's scent in the air. Not a fouls smell either. It was pleasing in fact to her nose. She inhaled long, and deep, with her eyes closed held it for a few seconds. thinking, "humph he actually smells good". Then let it out, opened her eyes, raised one eyebrow, smirked just a bit, tilted her head just slightly and said. "Mmm!"

She then started feeling around for her phone, looking around as did so she saw it on the end table next to the chair she was setting in. she grabbed the phone, dialed a number, a man answered, she spoke without saying who she was, "I just had a vision! And it was crazy, I am coming over you have got to hear this!" all the while grabbing what she needed.

She hung up the phone and ran out of the cabin.

Kimberley, Australia 5000 B.C.

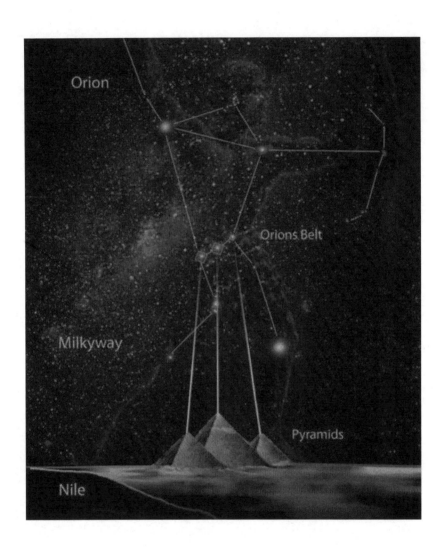

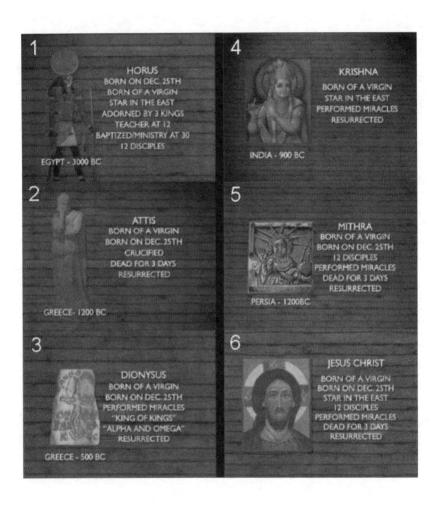

1

HORUS
BORN ON DEC. 25TH
BORN OF A VIRGIN
STAR IN THE EAST
ADORNED BY 3 KINGS
TEACHER AT 12
BAPTIZED/MINISTRY AT 30
12 DISCIPLES

EGYPT - 3000 BC

2

ATTIS
BORN OF A VIRGIN
BORN ON DEC. 25TH
CRUCIFIED
DEAD FOR 3 DAYS
RESURRECTED

GREECE- 1200 BC

3

DIONYSUS
BORN OF A VIRGIN
BORN ON DEC. 25TH
PERFORMED MIRACLES
"KING OF KINGS"
"ALPHA AND OMEGA"
RESURRECTED

GREECE - 500 BC

4

KRISHNA
BORN OF A VIRGIN
STAR IN THE EAST
PERFORMED MIRACLES
RESURRECTED

INDIA - 900 BC

5

MITHRA
BORN OF A VIRGIN
BORN ON DEC. 25TH
12 DISCIPLES
PERFORMED MIRACLES
DEAD FOR 3 DAYS
RESURRECTED

PERSIA - 1200BC

6

JESUS CHRIST
BORN OF A VIRGIN
BORN ON DEC. 25TH
STAR IN THE EAST
12 DISCIPLES
PERFORMED MIRACLES
DEAD FOR 3 DAYS
RESURRECTED

PYRAMID STRUCTURES OF THE WORLD v2.0

DESIGNED BY
SIMON E. DAVIES

ZIGGURAT OF TEPE SIALK
Kashan, Iran: 3000 BCE

PYRAMID OF DJOSER
Memphis, Egypt: 2610 BCE

PYRAMID OF KHUFU
El Giza, Egypt: 2560 BCE

ZIGGURAT OF UR
City of Ur, Iraq: 2100 BCE

CHOGHA ZANBIL (Ziggurat)
Khuzestan, Iran: 1250 BCE

TOMB OF KING KASHTA
Shendi, Sudan: 500 BCE

JEBEL BARKAL PYRAMID
Karima town, Sudan: 300 BCE

QIN SHI MAUSOLEUM
Xi'an, China: 210 BCE

PYRAMID OF CESTIUS
Rome, Italy: 12 BCE

PYRAMID OF THE SUN
Teotihuacan, Mexico: 100 CE

TOMB OF THE GENERAL
City of Ji'an, China: 300 CE

BOROBUDUR TEMPLE
Java, Indonesia: 800 CE

PRANG TEMPLE
Koh Ker, Cambodia: 940 CE

EL CASTILLO
Chichen Itza, Mexico: 1000 CE

XIA TOMBS
Ningxia Hui, China: 1045 CE

MORONGO UTA PYRAMID
Rapa Iti, Polynesia: 1450 CE

CHAPTER
10

Buggout!

SETTING IN THE MESS THE next morning eating some oat something, and coffee. John was still thinking about al that took place, mostly when he moved, everything was stuff, and bruised. At least nothing broken, or so they say, his nose feels like it could be broken, he had a few teeth that feel loose, a few ribs that the jury is still out on, road rash, and the back of his head still hurts! One of the girls sat down to his right, he did not have there names down yet as well as he would like, so he had to look over at her for a second to remember which one it was.

John saw the scratches, scrapes, and bruises', on her face and arms, he knew that this was the one they call "RAIN" she had a plate with what looked like the same oat something he had, a piece of bread, and a coffee cup, though he did not know it was coffee he was pretty sure. Rain was eating a piece of bread looking at her plate, her hair was not to long, though it was lust long enough to cover her eye's with her head down like it was. She said only loud enough so that John could hear, "You good to go?"

John looked back at his coffee, took a sip of it before answering with, "Rodger that", that asked,"you?"

She replied, "Good to go" then eat some of her bread.

John was reflecting on all that had happened from the time he was leaving work until this moment.

He looked toward rain as he asked, "that guy, that T boned us and pulled me out of the car? Had you seen him before?"

"No" was the reply.

John continued, "I fought that S.O.B. twice last night, I hit him with a ton of stuff, he crashed his SUV into us, you tossed him like a rage doll, he still had hardly a scratch on him".

Rain looked at him for the first time. She looked into John's eye's for a few seconds before answering, "Yeah, not the first time I've seen that either".

John holding her gaze asked" really? Any thoughts?"

She took in a breath then, "good genes, steroids, tuff Mudder, genetic enhancement, Hybrid, or just down right Alien, or it could be that they are just the lucky S.O.B.'s that go through life never getting touched", then added, "What I do know is they bleed just like you and I".

John hung up what she had said, or a part at least.

"enhancement?, Hybrid?, Alien?", "Do you believe that?" he finally asked.

She looked around the room. That spoke, "Do you see everything that is going on here?", she did not wait for John to answer, "It is not just this place, it is all over the world, there are a lot of people, good people, credible people, that are believing in this, more and more every day." she leaned in a bit closer.

Looking John right in the eye's said," I have seen some stuff I can't explain, do you see the tech. that we have?", "what you have seen in the tip".

Before John could ask her anything else, Jim came over with his breakfast, and coffee. Setting across from John, Jim asked John, "How are you feeling this morning?"

John answered," Like I was hit by a car," while saying this part John leaned to his right extended his right elbow, and gave Rain a small nudge. "Then hit by a SUV", "Other then that I am fine". Jim looked at Rain with a smile. Rain spoke, "you should have looked before you leaped dumb ass" a little smirk on her face as she said this told John and Jim she was joking. Jim still smiling asked John,"Any questions?"

John asked "this place?"

"It is ours John; Dad bought it years ago, from the military".

John looked surprised as he asked, "The military?", and then continued,' "you are not worried they will just walk right in here?" Jim looked at his brother with disappointment as he said, "Common John do you think that you, and I were brought up by a moron?"

He did not wait for an answer it was a rhetorical question. "First; Most of the government, and most of the military does not know any of this is going on, it is a shadow group", "Second; Dad bought it under a fake name"!

John looked around the room at the place, before asking, "Fake name?" Jim smiled as he said, "Yep untraceable back to him, It was bought by "Leonard O'Neill, Prepper, Entrepreneur, and Millionaire".

They all three laughed long and hard! "It is all traced back to the native tribes around here, all of whom are all people"! They continued laughing!

"Smoke! This is (Meltdown) how do you read? Over"

Smoke was monitoring this morning for any traffic and Julie "Jewels" Cohagon Aka, "Meltdown" had a convoy moving from the panhandle of Florida to south Texas.

"copy Melt!, how goes it?"

"Day two, clean, got news, need com. Base actual over?"

Smoke replied, "Rodger that", she then pressed a button and spoke "Attention, Attention! Meltdown convoy in rout, has Intel, for Base actual!, Say again Meltdown convoy in rout, has Intel, Base actual!"

Jim heard this over the intercom, looked at John, and motioned lets go see what is going on. John said, "You are base actual" more like a question and a statement at the same time. "Rodger that" was his brothers response as they got up from the table. They headed out the door, a few feet ahead was a staircase that went up or down. They went down, one flight, then a sharp left, and down again. In standard military base, or ship, or sub style, to optimize space. Then once at the bottom of this flight, they turned left again. Nevertheless, skirted the stairs to the right, and then turned right. A hallway, ten feet long, second door on the right. They went in. still seated at the radio, with a headset on was smoke. She saw Jim and John come in the room, she pointed to the spot that Jim would need to plug into. Not missing a beat Jim grabbed a headset that sat above the radio hung in the spot that had a name of each person that used the headset, Jim grabbed the one marked "BOSS" put it on, and plugged onto the whole smoke had point to.

"This is Base actual!" Meltdown knew his voice and did not need to authenticate him, she started speaking, "They have started a task force to hunt us! Say again a task force to hunt us! Over", Jim knew this was going to happen at some point it had to.

"How many?" he asked. "Thirty five so far and still recruiting", was the response. Jim did not flinch but asked, "Do they know our numbers?" Meltdown put in, "Negative, I am sure they are guessing, Sir you know this means they have at least same number ramping up in every friendly country?" Jim answered with, "Rodger that! We knew this was going to happen, I am surprised it took this long". "Rodger that Sir!" Jim put in again, "Do we have authentication on this?" "Rodger that Sir Came from the top, they will broadcast world wide in thirty Mic's, that is 3-0 mic's! Over".

Jim looking at his watch answered her, "Rodger that south mountain Base out!" he took off his headset put it back were he had got it from. Jim looked at John, then at smoke saying, "they have a task for, and are, hunting us now. they do not know our numbers yet. That means they will be ramping up all over the world to find, and stop us." John listened to what Jim was saying, then said, "This can NOT be about little green men Jim!", "What is really going on?"

Jim look more Sirius at his brother then every he had as an adult, "what IF it IS True John?", "Think about it for a minute", "If it Is True ALL of it or Any of it is true on any level!, Then they still are not telling the truth to the people!"

John cut him off right then, "Jim! If it is ALL or any of it bull crap! Then you guys! Everything you are doing! ALL of THIS (as John waved his arm around) is just Nuts! It is just a bunch of Rogue Terrorists or Rebels trying to pull off a coup!"

Jim calmed himself as he said, "John you are my brother, you of all people know me, you know that I am a Patriot! As are you, we are both in Military intelligence! That is out of the question, we are not that guy!"; "They ARE up to and hiding something! I think it is Aliens, and so do a lot of people"

"Proof!" was John's answer again.

Then it dawned on John! "Names! Names! Jim they have your name and my name!"

Right that second on the wall was a red phone it began to ring! Everyone in the room stood still, they all looked at each other in turn and back to the phone on the wall. "It has not been thirty minutes, and this is not a broad cast!", smoke fired in "it's the big boss!"

Jim pulled the phone handset off the wall put it to his ear as ha spoke, "This is South Mountain Actual over!" the man on the other end of the phone spoke plainly "Jim! This is Robert! You do know that they have put your name, the names of your brother, and entire family to this thing Right?" Jim breathed then responded "Yes Sir we are aware of that", Robert on the other end said, "We have talked it over; we need you, and your family to leave the U.S. to the safety of a base or bases elsewhere. Were they have less control", "You guys are now going to be the poster boy's for this. They will put you on every channel, you know this right? If you are not already. you probably have your own satellite by now or even two", "I do not have to tell you to move fast keep your heads down, and go low tech, Right?", Jim answered "Rodger that Sir!", "Sir? John is not fully on board Sir", the answer came fast, "Vet him in on what we have, show him what we know, and let him decide, if he wants out drop him someplace, we don't have time now to debate this, he either believes or he is asleep, copy?", Jim answered, "Rodger that Sir!, South Mountain out!" Jim hung up the phone, ok grab your gear people we are bugging out, he looked at smoke and said, "Round everyone up in the mess!"

"Rodger!" was her response as she pressed a button and spoke her voice cam over the base wide intercom. "Attention! Attention! All personnel EVAC MEET in MESS this is not a drill! Say again NOT A DRILL this is REAL WORLD, EVAC MEET IN MESS ASAP!" she took off her head set put it in the spot that her headset goes and followed the two brothers as they all ran to the mess hall.

It did not take long for everyone to make there way to the mess hall after all this was just a old nuclear missile silo not a real base, currently they only have thirty personnel here, that is more then the place can sustain if they had to lock down air tight.

Jim talking load so everyone can hear him,"OKAY! Can everyone hear me in the back?" He looked at the people in the back; they all nodded that they could hear him. He continues, "Listen up! This just in from high up!, they are going to if not already using myself, my brother, Mother, and Fathers name plastered all over social media, we probably have our own spy satellites! The four of us have been ordered to evacuate the United States ASAP! By Low Tech means. We will Rendezvous with fleet outside of the U.S.", "Peabody" Sherman Kolinsky spoke up, "What does that mean? Low tech evac, and how can that be ASAP?" this was a good question in a time of all the technology we have in this world. Everyone knew this, and you could see the looks on every one faces that said the same thing.

Then "wind walker" Daniel Breakwater native American raised his hand. Jim saw him, and quitted the murmuring in the mess hall with a word, "Daniel?"

Everyone went silent, they all looked at Daniel standing there with his hand raised, as soon as the murmur stopped Daniel spoke, "I have an Idea".

CHAPTER 11

Into the spotlight

"CHIEF!", "THEY ARE COMING IN from every place now!"

The Man was saying to the head master chief at the Emergency counsel called in the U.S. only for the second time any one could remember, it was hard to call an emergency counsel, hide it, keep it secret, and keep media out, or it was until natives could have casinos on reservations' there was a time that native Americans from at least twenty different tribes got together in one place at the same time in the U.S. even if it was on tribal land. Now everyone shows up to a casino way out in the desert no one seemed to pay much attention. In this case it was a good thing.

"we have a delegate from almost every tribe".

At first they interviewed individual tribes one at a time, in no time at all it was very apparent that this was not necessary any longer as the story was for the most part the same word for word the same story coming in from all across the Americas. A vision of the ancient Ant people saving their tribes by hiding them under ground in large caves, that they could live in, according to mythos did live in, for some ten thousand years before reemerging. This took place in the past, thousands of years ago. All they had to do now was figure out why they are all seeing this now? Is this the same thing from before? Is this a new vision of future events? And why? All without scaring the population, all without the American government finding out about it.

"Easy task!" thought Chief White cloud head of all this craziness.

"Okay colonel, so what is going on fully at this point?" asks Admiral Bares as he walks up to colonel Timothy Poe USMC who was standing an the war room of the newly formed "Home land special operation" unit looking at all the screens down in the pit. Col. Poe answers with, "well Sir we have Total autonomy to go every place at any time for no reason, and do what ever we wish any ware in the world, we have every thing at are disposal and I mean everything every ware all the time we have priority!" the Admiral looked into Poe's eyes for a second then spoke, "wow! Really? Nice, do we have any idea of the numbers they have?". Poe answered "Well just the two brothers Jim, and John both in High level top secret military Intelligence departments so vetted that they could not tell each other what they did, the father Francis was a lifer in high Intel placement, we have no idea really how long this was going on", then he continued, "The fact that the father is in on it, could say this has been going on for a generation or at least twenty years, if that be the case how many do you think are involved?, and how big could it be?"

The Admiral asked another question, "How did we not see this?" Poe looked not at the Admiral he just continued looking at the screens as he said, a bit more quietly, "This program has been in place and shut down many time Sir, for more then sixty years, are you not aware of that?" the Admiral replied, "Smoke and mirrors Colonel!, Smoke and mirrors!"

Then Asked the Hard Question, "With all that we got, with every thing at are disposal you are telling me that we have to this point NO idea ware they are? AT ALL?" the answer did not come from the Colonel, to his left it came from the Admiral right, both men looked to see who was first eve dropping and second interjecting in the conversation like as if it was a discussion at the water cooler. LT. Tina Collens USAF once again piping in when she should not, and once again with words that made them forget protocol.

Daniels idea was sound, "vehicles packed and ready to go Sir!" one of the men Jim did not know as well was saying, "Joe right?" Jim asked "Yes Sir" was the response "You able to hold this place son?"

"To the death sir!" Jim patted him on the back and said "Lets hope it never comes to that Joe"

Joe looked him in the eye and said "Our freedom and independence is far more worth the fight sir!"

Jim smiled while looking over at John, who was himself a bit proud, "both at the same time answered Joe with "Rodger that!"

Everyone was ready waiting for Jim, he looked at the whole scene hoping this would not be the last time he saw every one assembled here, "OK vehicle one is driver Kendle, shot gun Ron, tech, medic, Doc you are both meltdown is not back yet, Mom and dad. Vehicle two driver, Daniel, shotgun Drake, general mayhem Rain, tech Ben(Ben Sherman AKA Blackbird in a native American possibly a cousin to Daniel however no one has asked), John and myself. Any questions?"

"Okay! Lets mount up and get moving, if we stop for gas or any reason all the McKandle's do not show are faces period understood?" every one at the same time "Rodger that!"

At this they all pilled in the vehicle they are assigned to, off they drove north by north west to the four corners, and Hopi, land ASAP.

Meltdown looking at the horizon, in the shotgun position, full black tactical gear, it did seam to be what most of the guys wore unless needed she was thinking. Her stomach started growling, then she had realized she had to use the rest room, her bladder was full. "Blade! How are we on fuel?", Blade glanced down and back to the road, as he answered, "running on empty, we have 20 miles according to the vehicles onboard computer". Meltdown sighed with relief, "Good

I gotta hit the head, and I am starving, "Cargo" How about you?"
"Rodger that" came the reply from Karlie (Cargo) Gustafson who got
the nick name from her name Karlie, and Gustafson Kar-Gu, cargo,
it was basic training and a drill sergeant said her name sounded like
she was goofing off so he named her cargo at least he said "It would
sound like you are doing something" and it stuck.

"Gas Food next stop!" came the normally quite "Blade" not sure
how he got that name no one ever asked, he did look a bit like the
actor that plaid Blade in the movies, Meltdown did not what to know,
if THAT was why or how he got the name.

The music was far to load, Bobby could barley hear anything
other then the music, and Billy was driving way, way to fast again,
he does this every time he is drinking! This car he spent so much
time and money fixing up 1972 Chevy Nova, with a 350 in it, the
paint was the last real thing to be redone, it was mostly primmer grey
these days. "Billy! You need to slow down man!" Bobby screamed
at this point.

Billy looked over at him with a smile and yelled back "What!"
then laughed, took a drink of his 40 oz. bud he had between his legs,
put it back between his legs, and started head banging to the music.
Even buzzed as he was Bobby was not dumb, although he must be
for getting in this car with him again when he is drinking, lucky for
him the town they lived in was small, but then that be why Billy did
what he did. or maybe because his dad was the sheriff of this county.

Billy took another drink, handed it to Bobby, and yelled "Take
a drink bro!", Bobby did then tossed the rest out the window bottle
and all. Billy saw him out of the corner of his eye and looked at him
like he just took his favorite toy and broke it. "What the Hell did
you do that for!?" he looked back out the back window then back to
Bobby, then the road, then the rear view mirror, then Bobby again.
He yelled, "that sucked!", then looked at the road again, then the rear
view mirror. he could see the bottle broken, beer all over the road still
fizzing. Bobby Yelled "Red light!!" Billy saw it but at that point had

to be doing fifty or sixty miles an hour, "Shit! Was all that he had time to say, he hit the breaks as hard as he could, he was not going to stop, he was already crossing the inter section, no car to his left, he got lucky there, but luck ran out to his right a black SUV, was crossing as they had the green light! Bobby knew they were going to crash had his seat belt on, closed his eyes and hopped that it was enough.

Meltdown was looking at the gas prices, when she heard cargo from the back seat yell "CRAP!!", as meltdown started to turn to ask her what that was about, A car running the light slammed into the driver side of the SUV going about fifty mile an hour!

The car hit the left front right at the tire! This would be lucky for the occupants of the SUV, any farther back it would be real bad! It was bad enough as it was, the front end of the SUV pealed off as the car's right front caved in most of the impact was motor to motor, although the speed was a factor as well. The impact and combined speed drove both cars into the middle of the intersection, though they may have been close to there when they collided, either way the SUV slammed side ways into the light poll on the center island with a great force, this caused the right side passenger door to fold inward, meltdown sitting in that seat impacted her head on the poll rather hard. Cargo in the back seat did not have a belt on and was tossed around the back seat all over the place buy the time the vehicles came to a rest she was out cold. Blade the drive took a good hit as the two vehicles ended up slamming side ways, he was warring a seatbelt. As for Bobby and Billy?

Billy did not have his belt on, it was not good for him. He did not make it past the first few seconds of the collision as he slammed into the dash, Bobby on the other hand did fare a bit better he was seat belted, he would live.

The vehicles came to a rest one of the horns was stuck on! Both vehicles leaked fluids all over the road steam came out of both, glass crunched under tires, most of the windows of both vehicles were broken out on broken in all over the occupants of both. The airbags had deployed on the SUV the drivers one had hit Blade so hard in the face it broke his nose, the passenger one knocked the wind out of meltdown, she was bleeding from a cut above her right eye she had got from the poll. And a fat lib from the airbag. Cargo in the back seat was banged up pretty good hit her head, on the left side a cut on her face, some how she broke the pinky of her left hand, it was sticking strait up at the middle knuckle, she had probably broke a rib or two. All out cold for a few minutes. As they started to wake one by one. The team each took an assessment of them self, then started calling out to each other, sirens were nearing, people were outside the vehicle talking to each other and some to them asking if they were alright? Meltdown called out as she was trying to see with blood in her right eye, as she looked left "Blade!?"

"I am alive, I can move!", "Cargo!?" she yelled.

Cargo noticed her finger, she grabbed it with her right hand, Pulled it back in to the right place, pulled it out so the bone could ease back into place, then did just that, and let out a scream of lots of pain, with a crack! It was back in place so she answered through pain;" I am good to go!", just then did meltdown over hear a woman on the phone talking to someone saying "I am not sure who they are but they look military, they are all in black you know military style clothes and it looks like they have guns! No I am not going to talk to them that id your guys job, what if they are some kind of terrorists or something!"

Meltdown said "Crap!", "we gotta move!", "everyone out!, out!, out!" not sure if the vehicle that hit them was on purpose or not they could have hostiles next to them setting up or if not friendly's that think THEY are hostiles on the way, either way they were in trouble with a capital "T". "Radio's!?" "Any, and are they working?" as they climbed out of the SUV, they could see that the other car was just a couple of boys not looking too good. Each checking radios and of coarse none working, "cell phones!" she yelled as the crowed started backing away from them. She yelled to the crowed "Relax!

We are not bad guys, we are U.S. Military! She pulled out her I.D. and waved it for people to see, Relax nothing to see here back away from the vehicle please, get those boys out see if they are ok!", one the phones worked, it was cargo's she said, "Mayam!", "it is the boss" she took the phone and spoke, "Shamrock?", Jim McKandle was on the other end of the phone his code name was "Shamrock", "Jewels!" what happened give me a sit. rep.!" she told him what had happened Jim put the phone on speaker handed it to John tapped smoke in the next seat back, she was sleeping she jumped, looked at Jim he pointed at her laptop, as he said "Jewels, are you still with me?"

"Yes Sir I am" was the response, "Ok give me your co-ordinance off the phone's GPS, we will get a team to extract you ASAP!" smoke had the screen up and was ready for the numbers meltdown read the numbers off smoke entered them, "Got them" Smoke said. "Ok meltdown we got you position keep your phone on, and charged, we will call you when the extract will take place to set a rally point, Copy!?"

Jim said into the phone. "Rodger that Sir!" she answered. Jim put in, "as far as the locals, keep up your cover as long as you can", as soon as he finished Smoke spoke up, "two hours is best time for extract can you hold that long?", meltdown looked over the crowd as she was listening to the question, most of the people were looking like they believed her being military, it seamed as though they were calming down from the terrorist idea, and going into the save the hurt mode, this was good so she answered, "Good to go Sir!" then disconnected the call, and handed the cell to cargo. And said "Two hours guys!".

Jim hung up his end, "Smoke send a second unit in as well for back up, tell that team to get a ranking officer on the horn to the local pd or sheriff to squash any nerves". he looked at John and said, "Okay that just happened".

CHAPTER
12

On the Run

"CHIEF! WE ARE ALSO GOING to need to stop for fuel, and supplies", Daniel said as he looked at the dashboard.

"Distance to next town?" Jim asked.

"Coming up on (Gallup New Mexico) Sir".

Jim while giggling said. "ok but no accidents please".

"Rodger that Sir" was the response, Daniel knew that Jim was just trying to make light so they would not worry, he was worried though, everything had gone like clock work so far, no one captured, or killed on either side. This he a more then a few others would stay the way for as long as it could, there was no way they could or even would ever take on the government or the military in open combat. That was out of the question. The idea was to get evidence to make them tell the truth with no one getting hurt! Daniel was telling as much to Rain as they were in the store while Drake was pumping gas, They were getting food and drinks. "what if it comes to that?" she asked. Glancing around to make sure people were not close enough to hear then whispering. Also not telling that it had already gotten to that point in the past two days. "Shoot Americans?" was Daniels question. "Daniel, you are looking at this the wrong way, you are looking at this the way they want you to, and the way they will paint it in the press."

They continued to move around the store gathering things, looking around with there eyes to make sure they could talk freely. "what do you mean?" asked Daniel.

"you do know that starting in 2010 most of the big counties of the world told the peoples of those counties, England, Germany, France, Canada, Italy, Spain, all of the large free nations told the people Aliens are real, they have been here for thousands of years, they are here now, and the American government has been pressuring them all to not tell and not to tell Americans about this. They have control of the Media, they have continued to not tell the people, Why?"

Daniel stopped moving, his blood ran cold. "Do you believe this to be true?" he asked with a scared glance.

"yes I do", Rain answered.

"Then why?" He asked.

"That is what I want to know" she said as they walked up to the cash register. She finished with, "And it is not like we are trying to sell U.S. secrets to the world, they already know, what we are trying to do is tell the people what they should know, That the entire world knows, and they are being denied".

"Jim, I have to use the rest room" John said looking at his brother like he was going to wet his pants. Jim laughed, "your like a kid you know that?"

The laughed, for a second or two then John said, "I really do have to go", "me to" was Jim's response. "Lets go and try not to let anyone see us".

Looking out the window watching the cars, people, and goings on of his gas station was the past time of the cashier as every other day and time when people cone and go, so when the two men got out of the Black SUV, Joking with each other as they walk around the corner to the cashier's right as he stood looking out it was just like any other customers going to use the restrooms. This time the two men looked familiar some how, he looked them over as they rounded the corner, Then turned his attention back to the inside of his store, and to the T.V. that was playing. It was when he turned the sound up on the T.V. that is recognized the two men from the photo's plastered on every channel, he turned it up just a bit to hear it as the woman and man in all black what looked like military fatigues up to the counter.

As Rain was paying for the food the cashier had a T.V. playing behind the counter she heard it before she could see it, from the sound of it he had the news on. "Typical for this kind of gas station, the attendance are always watching the news or a radio with the same on". She was thinking as her mind grabbed hold of what was being said. {Fugitives! Broke out of a police, and military taskforce lock down of the emergency room at Iron wood Medical center in Queen Creek, Arizona two nights ago, rammed a road block, shot there way past that, and were picked up by a black SUV who's occupants got out with military style assault rifles, Opened fire on Law enforcement personnel! Escaping in an other SUV, and drove out into the desert.!} Looking at the Television while the cashier was ringing up the supplies Rain saw the pictures of both Jim and John on the T.V. screen. "You believe that?" the cashier said while moving his chewing tobacco from one side of his cheek to the other side, then spit into a cup he had setting on the register. Then continued without waiting," E'm two fella's worked for the military, They's some kind'a secret service, next level knd'a stuff, E'm Fellas said them boyz, turned commie, or turned Taliband, or some such Bull crap!, other then that Mcvay, Fella, aint been no (Mc Irish, schott,) every turned taliband terrorist! no sir, airs some other kind'a something' goin on and this fella is behind it" he jabbs with his thumb toward the T.V., all three look at the T.V. as the reporter is not interviewing "Cobb", "His boss is some hot number little blonde woman, name'a Tina something", Cobb was speaking now "They are considered armed and very dangerous, we know of at least five of them in this

90

cell we will be giving full descriptions of all Terrorists when we are done with this interview, as I said before these two men(the pictures of John, and Jim flashed back up on the screen) Are Identified as military personnel who we believe are a sleeper cell for a home grown terrorist organization possibly working with Isis and/or the Taliban, we would also like to speak to the parents of the two", pictures of there mom and dad popped up on the screen now along with there names. Rain realized that the cashier was talking to her again, thinking he was giving her the total she focused on him again, as he was saying, "see, that boy is bald, they are mostly bald, the move just a bit to fast and when things get them flustered or flashes from the cameras you can see it in there eye's".

Rain asked, "what?" he cut her off with, "Watch, whenever they end an interview like this they flash the pictures and all the flashes goes off, Watch his eye's you'll see". Just as rain looked at the T.V. he was ending the interview, and right on que the camera's flashed! They all watched the event unfold, as he turned to walk away you could tell that the flashes were bothering him, "Who don't they bother?" Rain thought as Cobb's eye's flashed something she had not seen before. "There! You'd see that?" the cashier said. Then he said "He is one of em!" Rain looked at the cashier then at Daniel, with a questioned look on her face. Daniel looked at her with the are you crazy look on his face, glanced at the cashier, then back, and made the that guy is crazy circle with his right hand, and pointed at the cashier.

However Rain did see something happen in the mans eye's, not sure what it was she worked at it in her mind and said nothing, other then "How much?"

They paid for the supplies bagged them and headed back to the SUV as fast as they could.

Just as Jim and John were getting done going, Jim on john's left, John next to the door, neither man heard the door open or close and both nearly peed on them selves as John though he saw movement to his right, he turned his head and a little seven year old boy was standing there looking at him. "Hurry up mister I have to go!" the boy said. "use the toilet kid Jim said. The boy holding him self now begin hopping on one foot. "common mister!" was his response.

John was done at this point so he moved out of the way, and said there you go boy. To witch the boy pulled up his shirt pulled his pants down to the floor along with his underwear, John said look out Jim he is going to Blow"!

Laughing John ducked out of the room fallowed close by Jim also laughing. "No parent at the door waiting, That is a shame" Jim said. Back to the SUV, just as rain, and Daniel got back. Rain warned, "we gotta go"! Drake had been done filling up, he was in the driver seat ready to go. As soon as they got into the SUV and got back on the road Rain and Daniel told them what they had heard on the news, Drake turned on the radio and turned on news radio, sure enough that was the topic of most stations. "Man we need to get out of this country and fast!" Jim said to no one, and to everyone.

The little boy was now in the store asking his mom if he could have a candy bar of some kind, when the T.V. was going, he could hear it but not see it as he was too short to see it, his mom was at this point talking to the cashier about directions or a map, the cashier point to a rack behind he and said every map you want is right there mayam, she turned and moved to the maps, as she did this the boy hopped up as high as he could to see the T.V. he could here talking about the terrorists, and the pictures of the two men the police want to talk to. Hopping again and again he could just make out the faces, though no details, he backed up a few steps and run at the counter, this time jumping as high as he could, grabbing the counter he held his self up on the counter and got a good long look at the pictures of the two men that law enforcement called terrorists. All excited now, "I saw those men!, Hey Mom! I just saw those men!"

The cashier was listing to the news and tuned the boy out by this time. Mom was looking at maps as she had no idea how to get were they were going, trying to get to Albuquerque New Mexico, east

92

was they way she was sure but how far and then she needed a map of town, her GPS took a crap about fifty miles back her phone was not a smart phone, so she had to do it the old school way, (Maps). The boy at point trying to get mom's attention was pulling on her pants, and jumping up and down. Mom not paying any attention said, "I thought you just went? Was the door locked baby?" real excited now, he is sure that the guys he just saw are in fact the guys on T.V.

"No! MOM! The guys on T.V.! they were just here!"

Mom now bothered by the boy and all his grabbing, stops him from grabbing her and pulling on her saying' "Chris! Stop it! What is going on that you have to tug on my clothes so much?" finally she stopped what she was doing and looked down at the boy. Still excited he did his best not to make mom mad but make her listen., "The guys from T.V.! the ones the cops want!" she answered with, "What are you talking about?", Chris rolled his eyes at his mom, pointed at the T.V. behind the counter and said the men from the news that police want to talk to!"

Mom starting to really pay attention now, "what are you talking about?", "what men?" Chris pointing still to the T.V. said "Those men!", "I saw them!", "In the bathroom just now!", "look!" Chris was pointing out side now his mom looked were he was point o and she watched the two men getting into a black SUV, "Did you see that?", she asked the man behind the counter.

The cashier looked right into the woman's eye's, looked outside then back again, then said, "Nope, I did not see them at all, in fact them fella's look nothing like E'm two on the Toob, if you ask me?"

Then grabbed his spit cup and spat into it, looked at the boy then at the woman, he stood right like that as the SUV drove away looking into the woman's eye's, after about three more seconds he put the spit cup back and asked, "any thin else I can do for yeh?"

Chris said "Mom it was them I tell you I saw them plain as day". the Cashier looked at Chris then back to his mom again, re-shifting his chew in his mouth with his tongue. With this the woman was sure now that the cashier was not being truthful, not sure why or what was going on she decided it was time to get out of that place, she was now a bit scared for her safety. "No I guess we are done, thank you sir" she grabbed Chris and headed out the door, only to be stopped by the cashier saying, "UM Miss!" she stopped looked back over her shoulder at the cashier, who said' Forgot your change, and your bag!". she bent down told Chris in his ear, "go get in the car now!", she came back to the counter put out her hand for the change, he ask, "You what I should count it back mayam?", she replied, "No, it is fine I trust you", he said "You never can be to careful these days" she new he was stalling her, she grabbed the bag with her other hand and answered with, "It is fine I will just take it", he handed the change to her and said, "You have a nice day now", grabbed his spit cup and spat into it again, then put it back, and watch the woman all but run to her car. And drive off, while dialing her cell phone. The cashier talked softly to himself. "Some people are strange, but I saw that ol' boy on the Toob, and his eye's turned, yes sir they did, What ever it is them to boys is up to it aint no terrorist nothing, run boys!, Run!" grabbing his spit cup he spat in it again, played with his chew in his mouth, moved it to the other side, then said, "I think things are about to get interesting around here".

"Admiral we are getting a few calls coming in of possible sightings Sir"!, The Sergeant from the floor of the war room was saying up to the Admiral.

"They were kicked to us Sir because they seem to be valid possible real sightings Sir!" with this more people circled around the Admiral including LT. Tina Who took control right away "What do you have Sergeant ?", two separate calls Mayam" one in Arizona, a car crash, one car is an black SUV, with three people who claim to be military, will not give up there guns, dressed in all black combat gear, flack armor lots of tech, Mayam", she got real excited to hear this, "Get some people on that and I mean now!"

"what is the next one you goy Sergeant?"

94

The other one is from New Mexico, mayam, a woman says she, and her son say Jim, and John at a gas station in Gallup New Mexico headed north, Mayam"!, she looked at him with a smile, and said "GO!", "send some people in a hurry to check it out"! the one in Arizona, were?", ha answered, "A town called Duncan on 75 Mayam, also headed north". she yelled out to the floor "Good work people stay on it we need to catch some of these guys and fast, contact local law enforcement tell them to detain only! Repeat detain only! To not engage or interrogate THAT is our Job!".

Meltdown's Gambit

"PUT DOWN THE WEAPONS NOW!" was the yell from the Deputy sheriff who had just arrived on the scene.

Now standing behind his open door of his SUV.

Meltdown could hear people in the crowd speaking both on there cell phones and to each other, they recognize the car that hit them, and the driver of that car. As it turns out the driver of the car the one that did not make it is in fact the sheriff's teen aged son!

"Put the weapons down now, and back away from the vehicle!" the deputy yelled again. Meltdown yelled back. "WE will not stand down!, We are United States military Personnel on patrol for the Homeland security!, Your office will be receiving a phone call shortly explaining this fact!, Lower your weapon we mean you no threat!"

The deputy started talking on his radio Meltdown was not sure what he was saying or who he was talking to he was just far enough away that she was not able to hear him.

Just then she could hear another siren approaching, it was the sheriff! He pulled up behind the deputies SUV, swerved to the right and pulled along side to her left the deputies right side also opened his door stepped out, and staid behind the door to us it as cover.

More vehicles started filing in all but surrounding them, more and more deputies hopping out guns drawn hiding behind doors, sides of cars, backs of cars, a few with shot guns, a few with automatic rifles. The sheriff looked in the car window of his son seeing that his son was dead, he was only about twenty five feet away from his vantage point. I looked at Meltdown, with rage, sadness, and anger! "You killed my Boy!, You will stand down and I mean Now! Do you understand Me!?"

Meltdown said to the guys "Crap! This could go sideways real fast, do not, REPETE DO NOT shoot to kill, Is this understood!?" "YES SIR!" in stereo was the answer. She turn her attention to the sheriff and yelled back' "I can not do that Sheriff!, We did not Kill your boy! He ran the light and hit us!"

The sheriff was not listening to any of this, Grief stricken he yelled back. "Lies! You will put down your weapons you will do it now or we will fire on you!" all the deputies started fidgeting around a bit glancing at each other and back to the SUV were meltdown and the two other men were getting real small behind. Meltdown knew at this point she needed to control this situation fast of people were going to get hurt and she might loose her team.

"Sheriff! You are in no condition to be here right now or with a guy in your hand!", she paused for effect for two seconds then continued, "Do you hear me Sheriff!?, you are full of grief about your son! You are not thinking strait!, you need to stand down and let your deputies handle this!"

"NO!" was the response from the sheriff.

Meltdown needed to get someone to listen and fast the sheriff is going to pop, she was thinking.

"Deputies! You need to listen to me! The sheriff is overcome by grief and should not be in control of this scene! If you do not have him stand down he will open fire on us! He is not in his right mind!"

She looked at the deputies one by one in the eyes to see if any are listening to her or if this is going to go south. She could see most of the men and few are just scared, one or two will do what ever the sheriff does, however three are looking around and at each other talking to each other, she needed to get to them before the sheriff goes around the bend.

The sheriff yelled, "Do not listen to her!, you will put down your firearms now!" he screamed with such rage that spittle was flying out of his mouth. As he continued, "Put down your weapons and surrender at once or you will be fired on!", "you have ten seconds to comply!"

Meltdown was thinking, "There it was!" she quickly spoke to the deputies again, "Deputies! Do you see how crazed he is!?, He is going to shoot no matter what we do! You need to stop him before we shoot each other for no reason other then he is out of him mind with anger and grief!", "Do something before it is too late!". The sheriff yelled in raged still "Shut up!!, Put down your weapons NOW!!. The people on the scene that were civilians were all hiding now peeking at the scene as it unfolded in front of them. No one spoke now for a few long seconds as the whole scene became more intense, then a voice from someplace hiding a woman's voice called out "Listen to her!", then "Sheriff put down your gun!".

The sheriff glanced in the direction the voice came from, as tiers started to form up in his eye's.

"NO!!" he yelled looking at meltdown.

The woman stood up from behind a car off to meltdown's right, the woman stood still for about three seconds then starting moving around the car and started walking strait to the sheriff, she was an old woman maybe in her seventies meltdown could not be sure. "SHERIFF!!" the old woman called out.

As she continued to walk slowly towards the sheriff!

"Trudy Tailor! You get down!, and behind something!" the first deputy on the scene yelled at the woman that was still walking toward the sheriff.

"I Will NOT!" she yelled back. "Sheriff!, you are a good man!, no one needs to get hurt here, these people do not want to hurt you, nor do they want to be hurt!"

Another voice from somewhere hiding spoke this time it was a man" Sheriff! Listen to her!" more people started chiming in from all over the scene

"Yeah! Stand down!", "Put it down sheriff!", "Stop!"

The first deputy that arrived on the scene was back talking on his radio!, as emergency vehicles started arriving. The deputy looked at the sheriff and yelled to him "Sheriff! The dispatch received a call, they are legitimate!" the sheriff yelled back "I know I can here!" then; from behind the sheriff someplace you hear a little girl yell "DADDY!", the sheriff took notice to this real fast he looked over his shoulder to his left "JENNY?" he said to his left, the girl called out, "Daddy stop!" the sheriff now no longer pointing his gun at meltdown, lowered his gun and said "Jenny Baby how did you get here?' then said "Baby don't come over here" buy this time the old woman Trudy Tailor had reached the sheriff, when he looked back toward the SUV, it was Trudy's eye he met, she said in a soft motherly tone; "Sheriff, your wife and daughter are over that way(as she pointed toward the little girl), go to them". the sheriff took a good long deep breath in and let it out as he did he holstered his side arm, looked Trudy in the eye's then with tears welling up again nodded his head, and walk away to his wife and daughter. The first deputy called out "everyone stand down!", every one relaxed and lowered what ever weapon they had, with this meltdown said to the guys, "Stand down".

From a crouched position behind Meltdown came this from Cargo as he stood up, "Well, that Happened" and they all giggled if not sure if it was to let off a bit of tension, or the impression of Shamrock, that cargo was doing by saying that.

The Native American counsel had convened after listening to many shaman from different tribes all telling the same story of the same vision being had across the Americas, they are now gathering the elders of the tribes to present them with what they now know. "Do we now what any of this means!"

One shaman asked another.

The reply was as it always is, "We will take it to the elders and let them decide".

"We are one hour out Sir!" the driver reported to Cobb who was in the passenger set staring out the window looking bored out of his mind.

"cant was drive faster"? Cobb asked.

The driver looked at the odometer then up at the road as he said, "We are doing 110 miles an hours Sir!" any faster and we will be a mess if a big pebble kicks up, are chances of surviving a crash at this speed is zero as it is sir!"

Cobb mumbled so no one but he could hear it, "speak for your self".

In an underground military base somewhere in Nevada, Air force Lt. Tina Collens sits at her desk eagerly waiting from the search teams to report back was shuffling paper work while looking at the clock on the wall, when her aid knocked on the door twice them came in the room closing the door behind him.

He reported, "Mayam! There is an Hopi Indian elder in the waiting room, Mayam".

Confused she replied, "Hopi? What does this Hopi want with me"?

"He asked to speak to you by name Mayam". the aid answered.

Then he continued. "He said that it is about the {ancient ones}, and {the second rebellion}, he said you know what he is talking about".

This information surely moved Tina, "Bring him in" she said as she sat back down at her desk and made like she was working on something.

Returning a few seconds later the aid lead the Hopi elder man into the office.

Stopping six feet from the desk the Elder stood silent and motionless.

"Mayam Hopi Shaman: crow wolf of the northern New Mexico Tribe". the aid introduced the man then turned and abruptly left the room.

Tina did not look up at first reading from a file the same line she had read now four times.

The Elder did not move or waiver, his eye's fixed on hers were she to look up at him at any time.

"What can I do for you Mr. crow? Wolf? Or crow wolf?" she asked as she looked up from what she was pretending to do. In doing so she looked him right in the eye, realizing he was looking into her eye's as if looking into her soul, even to her it was a bit unsettling. Crow wolf paused looking at her for a good five to seven seconds before speaking.

Then he gave it to her all the way.

"two days ago, eight hundred people from ten tribes met at one of the casino's owned by native Americans on Native land. to discus the eighteen shamans, from all over the world, having the same vision, a vision about the Ancient ones, the first rebellion, and a second rebellion."

She held real still, looking deep now into this mans eye's before she asked. "What does this have to do with me and the U.S. military"?

Not wavering either the Elder simply returned her gaze. Then after a good five seconds again the man spoke, "Lets not fool each other" he said then continued after three seconds "they believe that it is coming, a lot of good people will die; innocent people will die on both sides! There must be a way to avoid this". Tina wondered what he knew. As if he could read her thoughts Crow Wolf spoke again, "I know many things, I listen to the wind, and the Earth, I know the old ways, but I do not want my people to once again be the brunt of the pain."

Tina paused now for effect for a few seconds of her own before she spoke. "what are your people going to do?", "And, what can I do to help"?

"Tell them all to leave the planet before we do something terrible"! not waiting this time he said. "It is not like it was before, WE are not like we were, it will be bloody, many will die". as she was looking at him he stepped back one step, in doing so smoke started to swirl from behind him, going in both directions at the same time around from behind getting thinker as it did so. All the while Crow Wolf was looking right into her eye's as the smoke enveloped his body his head was still visible, just before the smoke swirled around from behind his head to finally cover him altogether he spoke these words "It is Different this time!". as soon as the smoke covered his face all at once the smoke expanded out and away from the spot were the shaman stood dissipating as it did so. As she watched the man was standing right in front of her, and then the smoke, then as the smoke vanished so did the man. As soon as all the smoke was gone she ran to the door and flung it open, looked out at the Aid at the desk asking "Did He just come by here?"

He answered her with a puzzled look," No Mayam, the door was closed until you opened it, Mayam".

"Did you touch him?, shake his hand or anything?" Tina asked.

The Aid looked confused, and a bit startled as he answered. "Yes I did, I shook his hand, why? What is wrong with that?" as he wiped his hand on his shirt.

Then asked "What is wrong is he dead or something"? Tina did not answer that question however she asked another "Are you sure? You fiscally touch him"? the Aid was sure it was wrong to touched him but answered, "Yes I did he walk up put out his hand I stood, shook his hand, he had a good hearty grip, he even had calluses on his hand".

Then asked again "Is he dead and I an going to die"?

Tina finally answered that question, "No he is gone you idiot, not dead just not here anymore!"

The aid was relived with that however more questions popped into his head, "Wait how is that possible"? he asked.

Tina looked at the Aid for a few seconds thinking "right, that is the question isn't it?' then said get back to work, walked into her office slamming the door behind her.

CHAPTER
14

Running out of time

JOHN AND JIM'S SUV DID not get more then a few miles outside of Gallup going north on across the 40 to the 491 when they picked up police radio chatter about them! Listening to the scanners now Rain said, "sir the woman back there call the locals gave a description and direction we need an alternate route sir" she was on the laptop working like lightning,

It did not take long she reported, "Coming up is a left take it!" she said to the everyone. Jim looked at her, and asked, "can we track there movements"?

"Mostly yes as long as they sing out were they are....wait hold one sir"! she was typing even fast now if the was possible. Now everyone was watching her, even the driver was glancing in the rear view to get a look. Rain yelled "YES!", "some times this is fun!, GPS! I Love GPS!, hahaha okay sir all police vehicles have GPS so the can be located in case of emergency, so I hacked into the data base! We have every law enforcement, and emergency vehicle tracked" she turned the laptop around to show them, all eye's on the laptop screen, even the driver glanced back to see! On the screen was a map of the surrounding area. All roads and all first responder vehicles broke down by type. Rain said gloatingly "They can't see us but we can see them!", then continued with "God I love my jog!" Jim smiled then asked her, "what about aircraft?"

All eye's back on Rain.

She looked at the screen and said "Crap!, give me a sec"!

John could not help it, he had to laugh, so he did. As he was laughing without looking Rain punched john in the shoulder real hard, then went back to what she was doing. John looked at her still amused, and ask, "What"? Jim giggled.

"Okay I got it now" Rain said after a few moments.

Then followed up with, "As it looks like they have a few road blocks up on the major roads, a couple of guys hiding along alternate roads".

Jim asked, "and in the air?"

"it looks like they are not actively searching with air support sir!", Jim responded with "Okay then other then the military that we do not have eyes on we are good, get us there off road if we have to"!

Rain did not look up from what she was doing she just answered, "Rodger that Sir!"

Back at the car crash site; every one was being check out by paramedics for injuries, Meltdown was setting on the back of an ambulance facing out with the door open on the bumper, as the paramedic was checking her vitals, she was looking around at all the people still milling around. The boys body had been removed from the car after the coroner came, and did their thing. flat beds were loading the two vehicles up to hall away as a deputy came over to Meltdown "Deputy John Perkins mayam, sorry about all this craziness with the sheriff he is a good man".

Meltdown was not impressed. "where are they going to take my vehicle to deputy?"

He scratched his head as he answered, "Down to the impound here in town next to the sheriff station, here is my card with the address on it and phone number, I am sure you still have stuff in it you need and it does belong to the military, just let us know what and when".

Meltdown looked him in the eye, and answered, "Thank you deputy" with that she noticed a van pull up close by, both she and the deputy look over at it, he put his head down and said "CRAP!"

Meltdown knew by the number 7 with a circle around it meant only one thing! News Media! Meltdown said to the Deputy "I would rather not have my people seen in the 5:00 O'clock news deputy!" he responded with "I am on it!" as he started for the van to head off the News Crew.

Meltdown motioned to her crew to rally on her as she ask the Paramedic "were is a good place to eat around here and a hotel we can was up in?"

"Not to far from here down town is a hotel they have a restaurant in it". she took a chance and asked him, "you think you can help us out by giving us a ride out of here so we don't have to walk down the street with tactical gear, and weapons?" she looked him right in his eye's, smiled, and batted her eye's at him. He smiled back at her and said "get in before they see you" all three got into the back of the ambulance as he closed the doors before the news crew saw them, then he walked around and got into the drivers seat, started the ambulance, and drove away.

"Less then an hour is all we need, stay out of site as much as we can" Meltdown told the guys as they stopped in front of the hotel just like the driver "quite Paramedic Guy" as Meltdown referred to him as in her head. "Rifles slung over the back up side down as to make them small people!" Meltdown said as she hopped down out of the Ambulance, quickly walking into the hotel. They waved at the driver as they did so. Strait up to the front desk they walked Meltdown did the talking. "Can we get a room please?"

The woman behind the counter looked at the three of them all dressed in black tactical gear, a bit disheveled, some dirt, and "Lord! Is that a rifle?!" with that both Blade, and Cargo both turned around so they had there backs to Meltdown, there rifles were behind them not to be easily seen by anyone. They looked around the room to see if anyone was in fact paying attention to this woman.

No one seemed to pay much attention to her. Cargo thinking; "She must be loud like this all the time so no one really pays attention to her, thank the gods"

"I need to see some ID, I major credit card for the deposit, you cant pay either buy the card when you leave or cash and the deposit will be credited to you" the woman said to Meltdown. "Crap! I left all that in the truck" Meltdown said as she realized that she only had cash," It was protocol not to have any ID or cars of any kind. "I hear you have a restaurant do they take cash? And were is it?"

"You don't want a room any more"? was her answer.

Meltdown leaned in and lowered her voice as she said, "No I do not want a room now I just told you I left that stuff in the Truck, I do not have time to go get it!, is the restaurant open? And were is it! Please!" the woman chewing her gum looking at Meltdown over her glasses, with far to much makeup, perfume, and the way wrong color lipstick, pulled off her glasses leaned in a bit and hissed like a cat in Meltdowns face. Meltdown did not miss a beat, she leaned in a bit closer, pulled up her right hand, held her fingers like a cats paw, with claws out, and abruptly Hissed right back into the woman's face!

The woman still chewing her gum, smiled just a bit at Meltdown, then said, "Well alright, that way" and pointed to her left. Meltdown said "Have a nice day", and walked to her right the way the woman had pointed. A hallway was in that direction, they took it. Half way down the hallway was a sign the read: "Kettle pot restaurant" with a hand pointing to the right.

Rounding the corner they saw it was a restaurant all right not that many people in it, in fact it was a bit dark, though that would play to there interest at this point, café style, with booths, and tables. As they entered the restaurant a woman from across the place said "seat your selves Hun, I will bring menu's"

That worked just fine for Meltdown she waved to the woman as they found seats strait in as far back as they could go and still face the door. Tucking there rifles in the booth as best they could they all sat. "Thirty minutes" looking at her watch, Meltdown said low enough so no one could hear but the team.

Cargo spoke asking a good question, "What do we do if they get here before are people do"?

Then fallowed with, "I mean do we engage"?

Meltdown took a deep breath, and let it out before answering, "only if we have to, lets hope it does not happen, in the open, in town, this could all go real sideways if that happens real fast". then she looked at blade and said, "Check in, give them are position, and situation. Fine out and updated E.T.A."

"Rodger that" was all he said, pulling out his phone and dialing.

Meltdown looked back at Cargo, "We do not want to get anyone killed, at all! It is going to come to it sooner or later, it came close a few times and we will be making that decision in less then 30 minutes unless they get to us first"!

She then continued "either way it is coming to that! Are you ready for what is coming?"

Cargo stared at her for a few seconds then said, "It is our! Planet!"

To which Meltdown replied, "Good Girl".

The waitress walked up just then with menu's asking "Can I get you guys some waters, soda, tea, or coffee"?

Meltdown answered her question with a question, "How far is the sheriff station from here"?

"It is just across the street" was her reply.

"And the impound lot they take cars to"?

The woman did not skip a beat, "right behind the sheriff station".

"thank you but no we are good, thank you for the information" Meltdown said as she looked at the other two, "I think we need go". Cargo looked up at the waitress and said, "Thank you mayam, you have a lovely restaurant".

The waitress said "thank you, you guys have a nice day" then retreated back behind the counter.

"okay lets move!" Meltdown said as they all got up, and headed for the door. Blade closed his phone and said "E.T.A. twenty minutes".

"Sir! The vehicle is at the sheriff impound, located behind the sheriff's office, which is located in the center of town on main street". Cobb glanced at the driver of the SUV, and asked, "E.T.A."?

The driver keeping his eye's on the road said "five minutes sir"!

"Good"!, "lets get these guys, I want people alive if possible"! Cobb said with a smile on his face.

CHAPTER
15

Cat and Mouse

"GOING TO HAVE TO GO off road sir, they will have us blocked in up here if we do not"! Rain called out.

"Do it ! Do what ever we need to do"! Jim answered and then continued with, "Are they tracking us in some way"? to which Rain, watching the screen called out "Left turn coming up dirt road! GO!" off road they went! "Going to get rough for a wile sir"!

Daniel called out as he turned off the main road on to the dirt.

After watching the tracked search vehicles on the screen for a few more seconds Rain finally answered the question Jim had asked. "No I think they are just getting lucky sir!" then followed up with, "We are now kicking up dust sir, they can see that from a long way off Sir"! Jim was aware of this fact he answered, "I know! Just get us to that rock formation up ahead, then we can reduce speed and cause less dust up, however we can't be out in the open, and driving at five miles an hour the choppers will spot us!" John thinking "That is a good call little brother"

Rain still fixed on the monitor, "We should be fine once we reduce speed they do not seen to notice us at all". Jim called out to Daniel, "Once we get to that rock formation and reduce speed we turn north again!", Daniel responded, "Rodger that sir"! Drake was watching the sky in every direction just to be safe asked Jim "Are you sure we are able to jam all tracking devices they have sir"?

It was Rain that answered not Jim, "Relax! Drake! I am on the case! They got nothing!", Drake looked at her in the rear view mirror, not looking up from the computer screen, Rain could feel his eye's looking at her, she flipped him the middle finger. John seeing this could not help but laugh, Rain looked away from the screen with her eye's only, looked right into John's eye's, raised one eyebrow, while a tinny smirk came across her face. It was then John fully realized that he was attracted to her. John then wondered if she had a "some one" some place. "Slowing!" came the call from Daniel as he did so he called out again "Turning North sir"! "Rodger that!" was Jim's response.

Pulling into the Airplane grave yard was Vehicle number one on board was driver Kendle, shotgun was Ron, Medic and electronics was Doc, and the McKandle MOM and DAD, they had the easies trip, completely un-eventful, they had made the best time.

"we just need to find the main building" Kendle said.

"Their" Ron pointed off to the left a bit. "Rodger that!" Kendle responded as he turn to his left, pulled into what looked like a parking lot, and parked in front. "Okay Boys and girls we have arrived at are destinations please put all seats back in the fully up right position, all try tables close, and be careful retrieving bags from the over head compartments". Ron said with a big smile on his face. Kendle not to be out done followed up with, "Thank you for flying we need to get the Hell out of doge city Airlines! We hope you had a nice trip"! every one in the vehicle broke out in laughter at this.

Before the laughter stopped, or Kendle could turn off the SUV, they heard something, like a motor off to the right! everyone in the SUV looked to the right!

Coming around the corner out of a cloud of dust was a quad runner! On it was a older looking Native American Man with long hair. He stopped just past the back of the SUV so he could see the driver. He called out to Kendle "Follow!"

Kendle said to the guys in the SUV, "Okay here we go!" he backed up as the quad took off to his right, he followed the quad as it rounded the building.

Just up ahead of them was a very big, and very old from the forties or fifties, an airplane hangar! The quad with the Native American was heading strait for it! As they pulled into the hanger they all reviled in how big the hanger was even father McKandle who was a lifer in the military had been in big hangers before, however this old hanger was in fact with out a doubt the marvel of all hangers. He spoke out, "I heard they used to make them this big, I have never seen one though until now!" Even buy today's standards it was considered big. In front of them were nothing just hangar, that is were they parked, to there left was not one but two mint condition B-25 Mitchell's and a fuel truck. "Wow!" They all had the same look in there eye's, as those words cam out of Ron's mouth. Everyone climbed out to get a better look. The native man hopped off the Quad runner walked over to stand in front of everyone. He then said" Okay, you are all in plane number one, that is the one closest to us, get your gear, load it onto the plane and we wait in the plane for take off".

Kendle asked, "Are we flying out soon?"

To which the native man answered, "no we leave at dusk, but he wait on plane incase we have to leave in a hurry"

Kendle said, 'It is Hot, in here, it will hotter on the plane wont it?"

The native man turned and looked at Kendle, from behind the native man was a voice that said, "He sounds like a white man or a girl".

Kendle turned to see who it was that just said that.

Looking at Kendle with a great big grin on his face was Charlie "White Eagle" Kendle's cousin!

Kendle started hooting like a Native American, so did Charlie, they charged each other like two warriors', the rest of the team not sure what was going on stood at the ready. At the last second before crashing into each other at full speed, they pulled up, jumped into each other's arms like long lost brothers smiling, and Laughing!

Sneaking around the corner from the coffee shop to the right of the shop Meltdown's team ducked down the alleyway as fast as they could to get off the main street and in plain view of the sheriff's office. They headed to the back, turned left meltdown said, "Okay we go a few buildings down, then back, and across the street. We go behind the sheriff office the same way, come into the yard from the south, and make contact with the retrieval team on an ETA. Timing has to be close. We get are stuff, blow the SUV, get out with no one getting hurt, got it?"

"Rodger that!" was the in stereo answer.

They headed off up the back of the buildings, made there way across the street by just slinging there rifles, and walking like anyone else would. They rounded the back of the buildings across the street, headed back towards the sheriff office. Stopping just south of the impound yard, they looked it over with binoculars, so they could see how many people they had to deal with. As the girls were doing this, Blade got on the cell again to check in. Looking around with her Binoculars Meltdown saw something she did not want to see right now! Blade ending his call said, "10 minutes out" to which Meltdown said," That is not good", blade said "ten minutes is good, we can get are stuff and go", Meltdown said as she point, "not that, That"! The team looked at what she was pointing at! It was Cobb he had gotten to the site before the other team did, he in his SUV loaded with four men had just rounded the corner of the sheriff's office. Was now driving the perimeter fence, of the impound lot, looking in it and two guys looking around for the team. Lucky for the team they were still a couple of doors down the way. Meltdown looked around, then back from were they had come. "Okay! We need to lead them away from here, so we can backtrack, get our stuff, and blow that SUV! Get out of here, with no gunplay, and no one hurt!" Cargo with a smirk on her face spoke, "easy enough" as she screwed a "flash suppressor"

Also known as, a "silencer" onto her side arm. Meltdown smiled back then said, "And No bodies". Cargo fired her gun at the SUV, hitting it dead center of the windshield.

Crack! Something hit the windshield next to Cobb's head, little pieces of glass hit him in the face, and he jumped, as he was startled, the driver hit the breaks stopping the vehicle, Cobb looked at the windshield, and a bullet was stuck in the windshield! They all looked around to find who did the shooting, and were they are? Seeing this Cargo giggled as she shot the SUV in the front grill, two times, hoping to disable the vehicle. Now that she had the element of surprise! The SUV started steaming, seeing this meltdown said "Nice work!"

With this last valley, Cobb and his guys were able to see the team standing in the back ally dirt road right in front of them. With the SUV, still smoking they punched the gas, and headed for them. Meltdown said, "Here we go team stay together if you can if not the SUV is the rally point!" they took off back the way they had come leading the smoking SUV away from there own. Running down the narrow alleyway back toward Main Street the team knew they had to double back some how at some point. Three quarters of the way to the front of the alley, Meltdown started trying doors, as they did not want to end up walking down Main Street with weapons in black tactical gear! One door was unlocked she opened it, looked inside. It looked like a hallway to an apartment complex. Meltdown looked up and down the building, as she said "Nice! In here fast!" they all ducked into the door. Meltdown told the team "Head down to the other end of this hallway look for a way out to the back side not the street"! she waited with the door open looking between the gap were the hinges were, holding the door open to make sure the dummies in the SUV see the door. Right on que, the SUV stopped all the guys looking at the door she let it go and ran to meat up with the team.

Cobb said "There!" pointing at the door that just closed as he saw it they went in that building", then "Everyone out on foot, we need to let this thing cool down"! They all piled out, "teams of two"! Cobb said he looked at the guy that was on his side of the SUV and said "You are with me, lets go, you two, {motioning to the others} around back and the other side! No shooting if we can help it we need people to interrogate!"

Catching up with the team Meltdown said "hopefully they will split up, if we are real lucky they go one by one on us, but more likely two by two, we do not know if more are out there, how many more may be on the way, so move fast, and keep together"!

When the team got to the end of the long hallway, they realized that there was one more hallway, that lead from the end they were at, to the right was the door to the front, and outside onto main street. To the left was a hallway, just as long as the one thy had just come down. Going to the back of the building, and the bad guys were more then likely going to be at that door in a few seconds! Meltdown wasted no time. "check all the doors! Preferably one on the left but we need to get out of this hallway or go up stairs"

The team ran to action checking the doors. Cargo spoke up, "I say we just get the drop on these bums and head back! ASAP!", "I agree" was Meltdown's answer, then she followed up with "But this distance to the end of the hallway we would not make it before they drew weapons". At the same time on either side of the hallway, they found a door unlocked. Meltdown said, "Go left! Left!"

The team rushed into the door on the left, and closed it behind them as fast as they could. Just as they did this, the guys out the back door did in fact reach the door! Moving through the apartment as fast as they could and still keeping quite, they looked for occupants. The T.V. set was on they could hear it. The apartment was small, not much to the layout. Inside the door they were in a hallway that ran a few steps, to the left was the kitchen separated from the living room that seamed to be strait ahead, looked like a bathroom on the right side just past the kitchen and a bedroom off to the right of the living room. They made there way slowly down the hallway, no one in kitchen, bathroom door closed possible person in there, cargo get to the living room, clear as well so bed room and bathroom, she moves on to the bed room. She comes back out shakes her head no one in there, she look at the bathroom door then the liven room it was clear, she points to the bathroom. Meltdown put her finger up to her lips and says SHH. Cargo in the living room now see's a sliding glass door, moving fast she looks out, it leads to the community pool that is in the center on the apartment complex! She motions the team to have a look.

Cobb and his team enter the hallway see that it is a long hallway, he says get down to the other end fast but stay quite, the guy with him run down the long hallway looks right, sees the outside looks left, and see's the other two guys entering the hallway from the other end. He looks back at Cobb motions using hand signals telling Cobb that one way is a door to the outside the other is the rest of the team coming down the hallway, doors on either side like this hallway. Then he runs outside to have a look around. He comes back in, again signaling both Cobb and the other two guys now. Cobb see's the stair case to the left of him, goes in real quite looks up and listens, he comes back out into the hallway getting real mad now because he knows they are loosing them motions to the guy at the end of the hallway to start checking doors and to have them do the same.

Meltdown says real softly, while motioning to the glass door "GO" they open the door, walk out to a walkway that goes around the pool, and to there surprise a gate that they so far have no bad guys coming in. they sprint the distance to the gate, look out, to then right and left, no one. "Do we chance it?" Meltdown thinks as she looks back, and forth. Her heart pounding now she knew they had to chance it.

"Move!" they exited into the back alley, turned left and headed back to the impound lot. As they are running along, they see the SUV that Cobb was in just sitting there with no one guarding it! They reach it look back down the ally they had gone down in the first place, back to the gate they had just come out of, and at each other.

Cargo says, "Really? They are not very smart guys thank the gods"! Meltdown says"Tires!, and break off the gear shift" with no time to loose the team slashes all four tires, while Blade reaches in and breaks off the gear shift then sets it on the hood and giggles. Meltdown while looking around again sys, "We need to go now move fast!" They all ran as fast as they could back toward the impound lot.

Inside the long Hallway as they were checking the doors to see were the team had gone, Cobb started to think. "Were are they?" he said out load. "Wait!" he said, "They are on foot! That means they are waiting for a ride, and they have to get there stuff out of the other one"! They he realizes he has all three other guys in front of him. In his haste, he sent every one in side, "WHO is watching the Truck!" he said rather loud. He also realized they did not have to chase them they would have to get the stuff from there SUV at the impound! They should have just waited there! Very mad now at his self for being caught up in the moment he just knew they duped him. "BACK TO THE SUV!" "Move! Move! Move!" they all ran back down the hallway heading to the back alley as fast as they could!

Blades phone vibrated in his pocket as the team reached the impound yard, he said "Phone" then stopped to answer it. They all stopped, each facing a different direction so they could see all around them blade was telling them on the phone were they were in relation to the town, what they needed to do, that the guys were hot on there tails. "Rodger that!" he said then close the phone. Blade looked at the two girls and said, "they are around the corner, we get are stuff blow it, they pick us up right there" he points to the corner of the fence, that leads to the front of the sheriff's office, and farther down the alley they are in. Meltdown wasting no time said, "Move!" they snuck into the impound lot grabbed all the gear they could find, and carry. The girls ran to the spot at the corner of the fence. While they did this Blade took out an incendiary device. Crouching next to the SUV, looking around he got ready to set the charge.

Meltdown standing at the corner of the fence looking both the way the SUV is to come get them would be, and back down the ally at Cobb's SUV knowing any second he and his guy are going to come running out, and that might be bad! Two SUV's came along side the Sheriff's office heading to Meltdown, her heart started pounding at first not sure, if it was her guys or more of Cobb's. It was not until Ron "Overlord" O'Graddy stuck his head out of the passenger side window with a smile did Meltdown know for sure. The first SUV pulled around the corner to the left, stopped and Ron got out, the second one pulled up and stopped just short of the corner. Meltdown motioned to Ron using hand signals telling him four hostiles back down the alley, Ron dropped down on one knee, pulled up his rifle and began looking through the scope looking for any sign of trouble.

Meltdown and Cargo hot footed it in to the nearest SUV, Blade seeing all this wasted no time setting the Device he ran as fast as he could to the corner gate, looked at Overlord, who motioned him to move to him, just then a Big Blast of white hot fire engulfed the SUV that Blade had just run from! Blade ran for it to the SUV Overlord had gotten out of, as he did this overlord stood up after Blade got in Overlord did as well and then sped off as fast as they could.

Cobb made it to the door just as he heard something explode, he just knew what it was, he ran outside and back to the SUV his team following, he just caught a glimpse of the SUV's as they rounded the corner at the end of the alley, turned right and got away. Cobb looked at the SUV in front of him seeing the gear shifter on the hood he looked the SUV over seeing the tires he grabbed the gear shifter and began beating it on the hood of the SUV as hard as he could and screamed as she did so! He hit the hood so hard he was denting the hood in! Once he was done, he regained his composure, pulled out his cell phone, and made a call. Whom he was speaking to the team did not know, they figured it was the base, and they were right but not to whom they thought. "We need to step this operation up! From now on, we have to have a bigger reactionary force, this is bigger then we first thought! Far more wide spread! I have yet to see the same one twice! What does that say?" on the other end of the phone was LT. Dean Stanton USMC who replied,"Are you sure?"

Cobb shot back, "Just in the past two days in the area of New Mexico, and Arizona. I have seen with my own eyes, twelve people, not including John McKandle. They have money as well, as good technology, And I mean good Tech. they have wrecked two vehicles, like they have plenty more! So yes I am sure!" he paused for a few seconds to let this sink in then said, "I also think they have tens of thousands, if not hundreds of thousands of people, not a few or a hundred like was first thought!"

Stanton listened to Cobb knowing Cobb did not over react much, If anything he down played most of the time so for him to say that many people got Stanton thinking. "Okay" Stanton said then followed up with "Come down here, we will beef up the task force, and assume that you are right". Cobb answered with, "It is better to be safe then sorry sir! I will see you soon". As Cobb finished the conversation, another SUV pulled up while all holey hell was breaking loose at the sheriff station and impound yard Cob and his team loaded up in the other SUV and drove off the other way. "Okay Boys!" Cobb was saying, "We are headed south! I just got the word. We are ramping up this little taskforce we have going here to a global scale! We are going to Mexico!"

CHAPTER
16

Under the radar, a close look at the creation of the Human race

WITH MELTDOWN'S GROUP SAFELY PICKED up, with both vehicles carrying all the McKandle family safely at the hanger, with all there gear loaded on the two B-25 Mitchell aircraft the native American team was now topping off fuel tanks and loading a whole bunch of reserve fuel tanks full of fuel into the planes, so they can fly farther. John asked Jim "why the old buckets"?

Jim looked at him, smiled, and said, "Ah Brother, you should know the answer to this one already. However, in this case, I will tell you these babies can fly up to1,200 miles, and we have extra fuel. we can refill in flight, then can go more then 200 mile per hour, and the most important thing, they can fly as low a the tree tops. Therefore, we can stay under radar. We will not have transponders running, so we will be invisible. Now if we are spotted and the jets come a looking, then the jig is up". He paused for effect, and then continued, "ninety-nine out of one hundred people seeing one of these babies flying by low, in broad daylight say, "wow well you look at that old plane! They must be having an air show some place near by"! Right"! Jim asked John. "Good camouflage" John had to admit.

"Flight plan?" John asked Jim.
"We will fly from here to "Corpus Christi" Texas then we split up. That plane goes on to the Caribbean, we go to "Cozumel Island" to go to Playa del Carmen witch is about forty miles south of Cancun Mexico so you can see some ruins first hand. Then we will see after that.

Both planes take off with no problems, flying low under the radar, it will take about 4 hours give or take maybe five hours.

"With the time we have, John I want to show you some things on the laptop, and tell you stuff about the {Ancient Aliens theory}, so sit down and get ready to understand"
"Okay" John said, as he sat down Jim grabbed the laptop, opened it and primed it for John's viewing.

He started with, "Okay, if you are nor convinced with all the rigmarole with them interrogating you, putting us in the news as some kind of terrorists! If that does not do it for you with all the stuff going, on and how big this is or how big this group I am with is. Ask your self are we all acting like a bunch of terrorists plotting to blow things up? Or over throw the government? Do you think MOM and DAD would go for that? Ask this stuff to your self, as we have to sneak out of the country. No here is the way things got started. Scientists looking at all the ruins all over the world keep seeing things that do not fall into the normal in side the box standard way of thinking. At first, it seamed like simple-minded people afraid of the dark. Every group of people in every place on the planet have an ancient tail of the creation of the universe and of some god or gods, like the Greeks, the Romans, the Vikings, the Chinese, Japanese, even Satanism. The churches have tried to destroy all the knowledge of all this and the history of all the other religions across the globe.

This we know from history. Like for instance when the Spanish came to Central America, and Mexico they burned everything not Christian, this was the main practice though out time. They then would build there temples to there god on top of the old temples they knocked down. This is real life history one can see this in any book or web site, library, ask any historian."

John did not dispute this point, as he knows this is and has been the way life has been as it pertains to history and the people who concur a nation, from the dawn of time right up to and even now.

Jim continues, "Okay so you know that they have been still finding scrolls all over the place, we talked about the scrolls, the idea that those people were thought of as gods, at that time in that place, Right?"

John answered, "Agreed they thought so at that time in that place." Jim touching the laptop, brought up a picture on the laptop, showed him the picture of a man with what would look like a kilt on. Most races around the world have similar attire, the Egyptians; as well, the men wore an almost mini skirt type of clothing. He had long hair, a full beard, some sort of headdress, or helmet, in one hand he is holding what looks to us today, like a purse. In the other what looks like an acorn, holding it at eye level, extending his hand forwards as if giving it or offering it to someone. On his back, he has great big giant wings as if he can fly. Now if these people whom are ten thousand years ago making this image in a cave on a cave wall must have thought that this was important to draw. Right?"

John said, "People draw things all the time in caves even today".

Jim said, "Okay so if it was just some random guy drawing some random picture he made up in his head ten thousand years ago, a caveman, then all the rest or the world at that time would be cave men as well, ten thousand years earlier. Right?"

He did not wait for John to say anything. "Then how do you explain this?" Jim touched the laptop again, this time is showed twelve pictures of the same man, and carved in caves all around the world. with the only thing not identical was some pictures had the opposite hands holding the two objects, and most of the carvings have the man having a bird like head. These were all found in caves all over the world carved at or about the same time in history." then he ask John this "How did all the cavemen all over the world get the same fax or E-mail to copy the same guy in a cave? The let John look at the picture foe a few minutes. Then clicked the laptop again and said, "the Christian creation theory?" he showed him the next picture this one had two columns on the left side it said Jesus, on the right it said Horus, next line Jesus story written down two thousand years ago, right side Horus story written down five thousand years ago. Back to left said, born of virgin, marry. Right side Born of virgin Isis. Left side North Star, led wise men to him when he was born. Right side Eastern star led wise men to him when he was born.

Taken out of Egypt to escape the wrath or Herod. Right side. Taken out of Egypt to escape the wroth if Typhon. Left side Taught in the temple as a child right side Taught in the temple as a child. Left side Baptized by John the Baptist at 30. Right side Baptized by Anup the Baptizer at 30.

It continued with walking on water on both sides bringing back the dead, miracles, twelve disciples, crucified, burred in a tome, resurrected, had all the same titles son of god, son of man, messiah, the way, the truth, the good Sheppard, and so on.

"If that does not get you thinking?" Jim said as he clicked the laptop to the next picture, this one had six figures and all the stats of the picture before word for word are the same it had Jesus, Horus, Krisna from India-900 BCE, Mithra from Persia-1200BCE, Attus from Greece-1200BCE, Dionysus from Greece-500BCE. He let John look this one over for a while.

Before showing him pictures of so-called flying saucers, also carved in caves all over. He showed him the Hopi Indian's, from the south west of the united states of America, around the Arizona, New Mexico area. How they say there, people were brought to the planet by the sky god, or star people, and how the Ant people came down from the sky, to lead them under ground. To live for a thousand years. Some ten thousand years ago to save them from an ice age. We know that the last ice age ended some ten thousand years ago." Jim showed him the India Hindu Mahabharata, and the Bhagavad Gita. Each of witch tells the ancient history, of the gods that came down, and lived on this planet for a very long time. the books also told about a great war between the gods, and many people dieing. In India, these books are not fiction. They are in the minds of the entire country real history, that is fact, and happened. He then showed John pictures of step pyramids including the three at Giza Egypt, that have been uncovered all around the world some dating back five or more thousand years ago, all the way up to about two thousand years ago, and we are uncovering more every year some even in the U.S.

Then he showed a picture of the Giza big three pyramids form overhead and the constellation of Orion. How the three Pyramids line up, in exactly the same placement, size, and distance, to line up with the three brightest stars in Orion. A picture showing the three biggest Pyramids on the planet, and how they as well, all line up in the center of our planted, at the equator. Spanning three continents also mirror the Belt of Orion. He showed him that the Bermuda triangle is on the opposite side of the world from the Japanese Dragon triangle, how they are on the same Parallel line, how most of the so-called UFO crash sites that did not happen according to the U.S. government all happened on the same Parallel line. The three biggest Pyramids on the planet not only fit in belt of Orion but mark the center of all land mass, and are on that same Parallel line. "So a bunch of cavemen, with sticks, and stone, build all this stuff ten thousand years ago. By hand, some not having the wheel yet. Most with no writing skills did this. Yet they all scratch a picture of the same guy, they called there gods, and said that they had come from the sky. Or from the heavens, from the stars, and flew in craft made them to mine gold, diamonds, and other mineral for there gods. How do you explain this?"

Jim said, "Think about all that for a while, none of it is a lie, it is out there in the world for you to find." Jim waited again a few seconds then said, "Then we are going to land, and show you one of the places we are talking about". "Oh and, one last picture we can't answer for as well. He then clicked on a picture, of the overhead view of all three pyramids in Egypt. Top down view, showing all the buildings. All of the walkways, when looked at top down they line up, one hundred percent, and it is over fifty points. Ten different size structures. As if the entire area was one giant processor chip. Look at that for a while".

Not from Here

LANDING IN CORPUS CHRISTI WAS as easy as they made it seam, sneaking into a tinny little hole in the wall back water Airport controlled by there people, was convenient to say the least. So off they went again in to the wild blue, this time the plane with Mom, and Dad McKandle headed for the Caribbean. While the plane caring John headed like they had said to Mexico. About forty-five miles south of Cancun down the cost is a small little tourist town called Playa Del Carmen, they landed in the little air port with the towns name, the International Airport was about ten miles off shore to the east on an island called Cozumel. We will be visiting both places to see the ruins, John was excited to see old ruins he liked that kind of thing as it was.

After landing, they had a vehicle waiting for them. They got in as it turned out they needed more then one vehicle as the hole team could not fit in the smaller then they are used to vehicles they had to ride around in were. So only four of them would fit per vehicle. So John, Jim, Rain. this trip, Joe "surfer" Jones road shotgun, the other vehicle had Blade driving, with Drake as shotgun, Cargo on tech. Meltdown on command, and mayhem after the ordeal they had in new Mexico. They were sent to meat us at Corpus Christi to fly out of county as well. John thought I guess if they are looking for all of us having us in the same place is easier to hide then all of us in separate places. Far less security that is for sure.

No longer warring the black tech gear the whole team was dressed like tourists running around checking out the sites, drinking, partying, and just having fun. Though the truth was that all the stuff that Jim had showed John was weighing heavy on his mind. John had asked for proof, Jim was making a really good case. Now walking the ruins Jims says, "This is small compared to the complexes I showed you."

John listening to his brother as they walked around.

"This is Playa Del Carmen, these blocks are not as big as most, they are still massive, and weigh many thousands of Tons.", "How did they do this?"

John started asking random people what they thought about Aliens. He was surprised at the number of people that said they do believe it is possible.

John and the entire team were so incognito and intrigued with the whole place, they did not notice Cobb as he walked by! Cobb was also dressed like a tourist, he was not expecting to see, nor was he looking for any of the team here, he almost bumped into John, as John with his back to Cobb was looking at a structure when Rain said "Wow guys look at this!" John started walking to his left as Cobb heading right at John while looking to his right tripped over something, would have crashed right into John, however John moving to his left made a empty place for Cobb to not bump into anyone, and right him self. Cobb looked back to see what he tripped over, by that time the team had moved some distance away from him. This went on all day they walked among the ruins John thinking about things asking questions. Looking all around, they even went across the water to the east. A few miles off shore, was Cozumel Island. Also, a tourist trap full even more ruins to look at. Before John new it, night was falling, he looked around; saw Rain, Cargo, and no one else. John made his way to Rain; he did not remember climbing this high. "Wow" John said the Rain, "I don't remember climbing this high"

Rain giggled and answered, "we didn't the Island is higher on this side then that, it is not as far down as it looks, see" as she points down to the flat valley floor at Joe who was waiting for them looking around all alone in the open parking lot.

"Let's hike down and meet him then walk back to the car," Cargo said. It was not too far down but far enough that it would take about 15 minutes or so.

As they walked along the trail, winding down it was very dark by this time. Johns Cell rang, he answered it, Jim was on the other end saying' "were are you?" "Are you ok?" "It's Jim" he said to the girls, then answered Jim, "I am with Rain and Cargo, on the east side of the ruins hiking down to the parking lot there, Joe is waiting for us then we are going to walk to the cars around the south bend".

Jim answered, "Good call we are above you, we'll head down wait in lot for us we all can go back together".

"Rodger that"! Was Johns reply.

As he was talking to Jim, John had stopped walking, when they had finished he looked up to see if he could see them above, could not see anything but blackness. As John turned to look at the girls, who by this time stopped as well to here what Jim had said.

John saw something out of the corner of his eye. He looked into the darkness and the mountainside, "What did he say"? Cargo asked.

Not looking at her John still answered. "He is above us will meet us at the bottom we all go back together" Then John walked towards the side of the mountain. "Is that a cave"? John asked

Both girls looked at John, then the area he was looking at. It was very dark, they could not make it out either; however, they all walked to the spot John was walking to. They all came together at one point, for the first time cargo turned on a flashlight; it was indeed a cave entrance. "HUH, I wonder were it goes"? John asked.

Rain said, "You guys up for looking?"

They all smiled, and headed to the cave entrance ready to go take a look. Like a bunch of school kids, they started getting giddy.

Just as they were about to enter the cave Rain looked back to see Joe, and make sure he was still there just out of habit. Joe was leaning on the light pole looking down kicking rocks. What Joe did not see and Rain did see, Made Rain's eye open wide, she said 'OH Crap!" Both John and Cargo hearing this turned to look at Rain who was now pulling her backpack off her back while looking away from them.

Cargo saw what she was looking at first, and responded in kind with Rain's remark' "Crap!"

John not wasting any time moved as fast as he could up next to Rain. As he did this, he looked strait at something hovering in the air making no sound, fully glowing a bright almost white, classic 1950's saucer shaped disc floating in the air! John could only say, "What?"

Before anyone could respond a Beam of light came out of the bottom of this craft, the beam illuminated Joe! Joe Jilted, and froze in place, in a way that looked creepy to John! Joe started to float up slightly! He was off the ground now by at least three feet! Rain was franticly digging in her backpack!

She pulled out a small rifle that looked like an MP-5 to John, However he cloud tell that it was not!

Rain aimed the rifle at the craft, yelled at it as if it, or who ever was in it, or controlling it could hear her!

"Drop him! Or I will shoot!"

Joe was still in the light, and was still moving off the ground higher to about five feet by now!

"Drop him! Or I Will Shoot!" Rain yelled again!

Joe at this point vanished, as John was looking right at him, John lookup from were Joe was to the craft! It was glowing more now! Cargo said in almost a yell "RAIN!"

Rain fired her rifle!

John flinched, and jumped at the same time as he had expected to hear a loud crack! The sound of a large caliber round firing! To his surprise, that was not at all, what happened! When Rain pulled the trigger of this rifle! A large bolt of what looked like plasma or a laser, or a laser/plasma bolt shot out of the rifle leaving the smell of Ozone in the air! However, the sound was not at all laud, with almost no sound, it seamed to give off a kind of heat. The bolt hit the craft! Doing a large amount of damage! Rain fired another round! Then a third!

The craft was not able to with stand three rounds from this, whatever kind of rifle was that Rain had!

Cargo Yelled, "In the Cave!", "Move!", as she did this she tapped Rain on the shoulder, to witch Rain retreated backwards looking in all directions! They all made the cave with no problem.

Cargo was kneeling with her backpack off grabbing in it for something, she pulled out more lights, handed them to John saying "Turn these on and place them around the room we need light!" John did what she said, it took him about 25 seconds, and buy this time Rain had taken off her backpack, handed it to Cargo John took this opportunity to speak "OK so what was that? And what is that weapon?"

Not answering either of his questions out right Rain instead said "Okay! I like you John, so I am going to say this once! I am not supposed to say anything to you at all; however, this is how it works! And the reason we are here with you now!" John replied with "I don't understand"

Rain yelled "Listen!, When you were created your DNA was programmed so that every person would never believe that any race exists other then the human race, and that this planet is the only inhabited planet in the universe!" she took a breath in then continued, "until you break that conditioning on your own! Then and only then will you be able to see the things you ignore. All the stuff your brother has shown you so far, has been there throughout time, and has gone unseen. Discarded, explained away, tossed out, destroyed, or hidden away from the population as a whole."

John's mind was racing now, with the images of what just happened!

Rain Looked back at John, as he did not say anything.

At that moment Cobb appeared through the cave entrance, as if he had been waiting for this moment swatted the rifle out of Rain's hands! Grabbed Rain, Tossing her to her left into the cave wall. Cargo with her hands still in the backpack on her knees looked up to see this going on. Before she could move, Cobb was kicking sand in her eyes, stomping on the backpack, and kneed her in the face, sending her over backwards. John joined in at this point, attacking Cobb, taking his back; John hooked an arm around Cobs' neck to choke him from behind! At that same time, another man came in behind Cobb.

It was a sure bet he was with Cobb; he punched John in the kidney, grabbed John, and pulled him off Cobb's back! The man grabbing John from behind like he had Cobb a second ago. John pushed with both feet to drive backwards, did so with good haste! He drove the man right back into the cave wall, very hard slamming the man in to the wall, and his body into the man at the same time. This loosened he grip on John, he was able to get away from him. As he did so the mans wristwatch that was on his left arm came off, during the continuing struggle they stepped on it breaking it.

Rain was not out of the fight at all just stunned a bit from hitting her head. She saw John working on that guy she went after Cobb again, with Cargo still getting her eye's clear of sand, she was no help just yet! Cobb had turned to see John, and the other guy going at it, he saw that Rain was still in the hunt. Rain came at Cobb again; she faked a move to her left, and moved to her right. Cobb was ready for this he stepped to his right, grabbing her left arm with his right hand. She did the same grabbing his left arm with her right hand. They looked like a dance couple, as the turned in sequence. Cobb tossed her left arm aside, reared back: and hit Rain in the chest as hard as he could! Mumbling something to him self that sounded like "ticking me off!" the impact of his punch sent Rain into the air! She was off the ground, moving backwards! One would think she was going to crash down, or on the wall behind her, he hit her so hard!

Rain seamed to move a bit in the air! She was not going to crash! Instead she went about four feet, witch was an impressive distance to be punched!

Rain landed on her feet, one leg behind her, acting like a rudder to balance her, the other directly under her. When she landed on the ground, she still slid a few inches backwards before coming to a complete stop!

As Rain did this, she was holding Cobb's watch that he had on his left arm. You see she bragged it while all this was going on! She showed it to Cobb, he looked at it, and to her with a questioning look. Rain pressed a button on the watch. Cobb and the other man had the same watch, the one he and John had stepped on. This meant, this, was the only working devise between the two men! As she pushed the button, Rain smiled at Cobb.

After pressing the button Rain took the time to step on it, making sure it was broken under her foot!

With this done both Cobb, and the other man that John was fighting, started to change. It was as if the entire body was changing. As this was happening, John saw that it was not in fact a change rather like an image fading away to revile a new one that was hidden below! New features started to take place of old ones; there skin was not pail pinkish like before. Now the skin was a green color, and the in fact had scales! They could all see them now for whom or what they really looked like! They were some kind of reptile race of biped! Two legs up right like a human two arms! One head two eyes'! With reptile eye's!

Cobb looked at Rain in what looked like a reptile smile and said, "That's right! We are not from here!"

Rain looked him in the eye and said, "Neither am I!"

Then charged at him again!

John head butted the guy he was fighting and found that was not a good idea, as he was sure it hurt him more then the other guy!

Seeing the man now as some kind of Reptilian! John realized he had head butted ridges on the mans head.

18

They are here

AT THIS MOMENT THERE WAS no more trying to say this was not real! John saw with his own what he now new was a flying machine of some kind either from this planet or from a different one! The men he was fighting are not human! In John's mind, it was like on the flight, when the flight attendant comes on the intercom, and says, "Please return to your seats, fasten your seatbelts, put your seats, and tray tables back to the fully up right position!", or when you walk into a crowded room. And the music scratches, stops, and all the people turn, and stare at you! Looking at the man who was by this time getting ready to bite off John's face! Or John thought that as he tried to figure out how to, or ware to hit this guy to hurt him! The Reptilian grabbed John and head butted him back giggling as he did this!, John staggered back a good two, if not three steps! John struck the man in the throat thinking, "He swallows when he eats, SO?"

This worked the man gasping for air staggered back away from John. Complete mayhem was going on inside this cave as all parties fought, struck blows, got hit. By this time Cargo got the sand out of her eyes, she was in a real bad mood for being caught off guard like that. She ran past Rain to help John, as she did this she made sure to punch Cobb in the side of his head with a spinning back hammer punch, so hard that he staggered backward with blood coming out of his mouth, and dropped to one knee! She continued on the help John, who was at this point not doing to badly! She did know that given time the reptile would win, as John has no Idea of the physiology of the Reptilians race.

Cargo smashed into the reptile hard, and fast slamming him into the cave wall!

Just then, three more people entered the cave! John could see it was Jim and two others! They had caught up with them!

Cobb saw this and knew they had to retreat and now!

Cobb grabbed Rain; head butted her in the face, turned, and through her at the crowd! Rain slammed into the crowd, knocking into or knocking each person into some one else, causing everyone to all but fall on the ground! Growling something to the other man as he did this, he grabbed the other man, pulling him along with him as they made there escape! Some of the team started to give chase however, Jim stopped them with a loud "LET THEM GO!"

Then "we need to get the hell out of here and fast" Jim then looked at John and said as much as asked one word, "SO!?"

John looked at him with a small grin and answered, "Aliens; WOW; OK, Now what"?

As Jim moved to the cave entrance he said, "we need to get out of here it is too hot!"

John thinking about everything that took place said, "I have a lot of Questions Jim!"

To which Jim relied, "It's about time!"

They made it down from the mountain with no contact of any kind ran as fast as they could back to the vehicles and headed for the airfield.

"Lots hope we can get out of here and they don't have a big base near by!" John looking around in every direction answered with a question, "If they do?" then this may be over soon for us" with this

Rain piped in with "Not! With out a real BIG, Fight and a lot of dead bodies we won't"!

They got on to the planes, got them running, taxied out, and got into position to take off when another classic saucer shaped craft right out of the fifties or sixties came in fast, slowed to a stop about four hundred yards away! Rain said "Cargo!" and started for the gun ports that this plane had. Both women had the weapons they had before! That looked like an MP-5 however was not an MP-5! Cargo opened the port; Jim yelled to the pilots "GO!"

They revved the engines up to full speed! The plane started moving. Cargo pulled open the gun port for Rain, who was not wasting any time, as she had her weapon up at the ready, just needing a target to shoot at! Jim yelled "Defenses'!" laptops were already opening and the girls were typing as fast as they could get fingers moving!

A Flash of light hit the plane at the cockpit right side! The impact, and brightness of the light scared the co-pilot, however did no damage to the airplane! The pilot and co-pilot both being Native American started chanting in native! Rain leveled her rifle at the craft and fired it more then once, twice, or three times John remembered! The craft was just gone! Lots of light then nothing! John asked, "Did you get it?" Rain said "Yes! But I think it may have jumped before I took it out!" they were moving down the runway as she closed the gun port they took off! Flying low, they headed strait out into the ocean, east away from Mexico and toward the Caribbean as one of the girls on the laptops said "we are clean, and dark! They can not track us!" everyone gave a big sigh of relief.

John once again looked at Jim and said "OK Lots of Questions!"

Jim laughed but responded, "I bet you do, ok we have some time on the trip! Welcome bother! There is no going back now!

Book two coming soon

At the Giza plateau: present day, nighttime, the team of Jim, John, Rain, and Overlord. Fallowing a lead to witness a ceremony of an Ancient ritual that had been repeated for thousands of years. Maybe even tens of thousands of years. The team is moving in the darkness dressed in all black using night vision devices to see. They are finding it very hard to navigate to the plateau it self, and see what is going on. As this place is locked down so tight with guards, that look more like secret service agents then not. Are impeding the teams progress. "We are going to have to look, and listen from a ways off guys," Jim says as he stops.

Everyone hold up, ready to do what ever the team leader say to do, in this case that is Jim.

"Ok get small people, we spy from this local".

Everyone found some form of cover to hide by or under.

After a few minutes of witnessing events so scary that the team did not want to speak about right now, they decided they needed to leave, and leave now! As they were making there way out of this crazy place, and the ritual they had just witnessed, they wanted to make a break for it! They had to hold up as many people seemed far to close by! "crap!" John thought!

Some one was real close, and moving in on them! From behind over taking them! Overlord looked the way they had to go! Rain looked to the sky, in all directions, Jim, and John looked behind!

An African woman came between two rocks looking back from were she came as if hoping she was not being fallowed. John and Jim took a glance at each other then back to the woman, John said real quite but for the others to hear, "A woman"

Rain answered, "Don't trust her".

As if she could see in the dark, she made for the teams position with most haste! The moon was not up, they are far from the city light by now it is pitch black out, and that is why the team has night vision on.

As she nears the group, she says softly "Do Not shoot me please", "I am in need of help, you must help me or they will kill me this very night!"

John whispers to her "Who are you, and why should we help you?"

She answered "You are the resistance I over heard you speaking", "you need me as much as I need you", "Please listen there is not much time, and we must go". She was saying now as they all were wondering how she could have heard them speaking? Unless she was near buy them, and they did not know it.

"They need to kill me, I am the proof! I am the DNA, I am the first one!"

With this Rain turned from the sky, looked at the woman, and repeated what she had said," The first DNA, The first ONE", she then asked the woman

"What is your name woman?"

To witch the woman answered "I Am Lilith! I am the first one"!

Rain's blood ran cold!

Rain looked at the woman but spoke to John, "John! Get her out of here! NOW! Everyone listen, if anyone, comes for her we have to kill them!"

John did not question Rain; he could tell something was really important about this woman from Rain's reaction.

Made in the USA
Middletown, DE
06 December 2016